As soon as she was in his arms she felt herself yielding to the powerful erotic sensations he awoke in her.

Slowly Randal pulled his head back and looked down at her, and Pippa opened her eyes to stare back at him.

"You kiss me like that, and yet you keep pretending you don't want me?" he whispered. "What's going on inside that head of yours? We're both free now, there's nothing to keep us apart—so why are you still fighting it?"

Note from the Editor:

Charlotte Lamb passed away on 8 October 2000,
at her home on the Isle of Man, U.K.,
surrounded by her family.

She started writing for Harlequin Presents® in
the early 1970s, and published 116 novels for
the line. More than 100 million copies of her
stories have sold worldwide. *The Boss's Virgin*
was completed just before her death.

Charlotte Lamb will be missed
by millions of readers around the globe.

Charlotte Lamb

THE BOSS'S VIRGIN

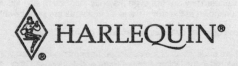

HARLEQUIN®

TORONTO • NEW YORK • LONDON
AMSTERDAM • PARIS • SYDNEY • HAMBURG
STOCKHOLM • ATHENS • TOKYO • MILAN • MADRID
PRAGUE • WARSAW • BUDAPEST • AUCKLAND

ISBN 0-373-12214-4

THE BOSS'S VIRGIN

First North American Publication 2001.

This edition published by arrangement with Harlequin Books S.A.

® and TM are trademarks of the publisher. Trademarks indicated with
® are registered in the United States Patent and Trademark Office, the
Canadian Trade Marks Office and in other countries.

Visit us at www.eHarlequin.com

Printed in U.S.A.

CHAPTER ONE

THE party was going to go on for hours, but Pippa was tired; it was almost midnight and she normally went to bed before eleven. When she was younger she'd been able to stay up all night at parties, but her body didn't have the late-night habit any more since she'd had to be at work by eight every weekday morning. She had been forced to realise that burning the candle at both ends was crazy.

She kept yawning, which wasn't surprising since the flat was packed with people and oxygen was scarce. She was beginning to feel quite dizzy as she shuffled around, dancing with Tom under flashing strobe lighting.

'Can we go soon? Would you mind?' she whispered in Tom's ear, and he blinked down at her, looking half asleep himself before he smiled that slow, sweet smile of his.

'I don't mind at all. I'm dead on my feet. Let's go and find Leonie and make our excuses.'

They found her in the kitchen making more bites on sticks: bacon-wrapped dates, bits of cheese sandwiched with pineapple, like the other finger food she had been circulating earlier. She hadn't had any help organising her party; she must have been working very hard all day.

'Sorry, Leonie, we have to get moving,' Pippa said apologetically, kissing her. They had worked together for some years now and Pippa was fond of her. 'We have a long drive back. It was a lovely party; we had a great time. Thanks for inviting us.'

Leonie pushed back her long blonde hair then hugged Pippa. 'Thanks for coming. People seem to be enjoying themselves, don't they?'

'They certainly do. Great food and great music. Where did you get that lighting from?'

'Hired it—it didn't give you migraine, did it? I know it triggers migraines in some people.'

'No, it didn't give me migraine.' But she had hated it all the same; the constant, blinding flashes of bright light combined with the loud music had made her head ache.

'Have some cheese,' Leonie offered, and Pippa took a piece, bit it.

'Delicious, thanks,' she said. 'Sorry to have to go. I hope you'll be very happy, Leonie. You've got a great guy there; I'm sure you will be.'

Leonie glowed, eyes happy. 'He is gorgeous, isn't he? And so is Tom!'

He laughed and she kissed him. 'I mean it! You are. I'm really looking forward to your wedding.'

'So are we,' Tom said, holding Pippa tighter. 'We seem to have been planning it for years. I can't believe it's going to happen at last next week. You'll be planning yours now. Believe me, it's a mistake to hurry. There's so much to work out.'

Tom was good at planning, drawing up lists, double-checking every little detail. He had masterminded their wedding; Pippa had simply attended to the details.

'Well, must go,' he said, and she followed him out of the flat into the faint chill of a spring night. She took his arm, snuggling close to him for warmth. The flat had been so crowded and overheated; the fresh air hit them with a blow that woke them up.

His car was parked down the road. All around them London glowed and buzzed although it was nearly midnight. On a Saturday most young people went out or had parties. The central city streets would be heaving with people drinking and laughing, spilling out of pubs and restaurants to stand in the road, talking, reluctant to go home yet.

Tom hadn't drunk much—he never did; he was a very careful abstemious man—but he had to concentrate to keep his wits about him as they drove through the busy streets which led through the West End and the grey, crowded streets of the much poorer East End into the eastern suburbs. At last, though, they came to the road leading to rural Essex, and within twenty minutes were a short distance from Whitstall, where they both lived.

A small Essex town with a busy market once a week, it had once been a remote village, a cluster of small cottages around a pond, where cattle had stood up to their knees, drinking, a medieval church with a white-painted wooden spire, and a couple of traditional pubs. They drank at The Goat, whose new sign suggested devil worship, although the name actually related to the goats which had once been kept on the common. The King's Head had a very old sign: a mournful Charles the First swung to and fro in the wind above the door.

During this century the village had grown into a town as the railway, and then the advent of the motor car, encouraged people from inner London to move out into the country. With new people had come more houses, circling and doubling the old village centre.

Tom had arrived first and bought a new house on a small modern estate which had been built. Pippa had come to his house-warming party and fallen in love with Whitstall, so she had bought herself a cottage there, too.

'We'll be home soon now,' Tom murmured.

Pippa yawned beside him, her chestnut hair windblown around her oval face and her slanting green eyes drowsy. 'Thank goodness! Mind you, I enjoyed the party. It's great to see our colleagues letting their hair down now and then. They're usually concentrating too hard to smile much.'

'It was fun,' he agreed. 'Leonie and Andy seemed to be on top of the world—she's very happy, isn't she? Getting engaged suits her.'

'Suits me, too,' Pippa said, chuckling.

He laughed, reaching a hand across to touch one of hers, the hand which bore his ring, a circle of little diamonds around a larger emerald. 'Glad to hear it. It certainly suits me. Being married will be even better.'

'Yes,' she said. At last she would be part of a family; she couldn't wait.

The street lamps had ended. They were driving along narrow, dark country roads between hawthorn hedges beyond which lay fields full of black and white cows which had a ghostly look as they moved, flickering and dappled, over the grass they grazed on. Here and there one saw a frilly-leaved oak tree, or an elm vaguely outlined against the night sky.

Pippa sleepily thought about her wedding dress, which would soon be finished. The village dressmaker was hardly what you could call rapid—indeed she worked at a sloth's pace, whenever she felt like it,

Pippa had decided—but the dress was exquisite, a vision of silk and pearls and cloudy fullness. Pippa had a final fitting tomorrow morning. She couldn't take time off work; her fittings had to happen at weekends. Of course, Tom had never glimpsed the dress; everyone insisted that that would mean bad luck.

She already had her veil, but she had yet to buy the coronet she would wear to hold her veil down. She had been looking for exactly what she wanted for weeks, without success. Then on Friday evening, as she'd walked to the tube station, she had seen a coronet of pearls and amazingly lifelike white roses in a wedding shop in Bond Street. Unluckily the shop had shut at six o'clock, so she hadn't been able to buy it. She would go back on Monday, during her lunch hour.

It had taken months to plan everything. She had often wished she had a mother to help her, but, being an orphan without any relatives, she had had to manage alone. The wedding had eaten up half her savings as she had no family to pay the costs. Tom had generously insisted on paying half, making himself responsible for the reception, the white wedding cars and the flower arrangements in the church.

Her green eyes slid to his profile, half in shadow, half lit now and then by moonlight, showing her a straight nose, floppy fair hair, a still boyish face. He was a wonderful man: tender, caring, warm-hearted. She had known him for four years and the more she learnt about him the more she liked him.

And yet... She sighed. And yet, she was still uncertain, troubled. He had first proposed two years ago, but she had gently refused that time, and the next two times he had asked her to marry him. Marriage was an important step; it meant far more than living together, or sharing a bed. She hadn't had a family or a home as a child. She had been brought up in foster care, never feeling she belonged to anyone, or anywhere, envying other children who had parents who loved them.

She had no idea who her parents had been, in fact. She had been left outside a hospital one rainy spring night. Nobody had ever come forward with information about her background. Enviously she had watched other children at school who had a family, a home, something she was never to know.

In consequence she took marriage and family very seriously. To her, marriage meant committing to spending the rest of your lives together, and she wasn't sure she could face that with Tom.

Oh, she liked Tom a lot, found him very attractive, knew him well. He was her boss. They had worked together every day in the same London office for four years, and had always had a good working relationship. Pippa enjoyed his company; he was a good-looking man, and when he kissed her or touched her she wasn't repulsed. If they had not slept together it was because Tom had never insisted. Oh, they had come close to it, yet he had always drawn back, saying he wanted to wait until they were married. He wanted their marriage to mean something deeply important, and she was impressed by his personal integrity. She saw marriage in the same light. Sex was easy. A life commitment was hard.

And yet... She gave another sigh. And yet, something was lacking between them. She knew very well what it was: that vital ingredient. She had been honest with Tom from the beginning, telling him the truth about how she felt. She was not in love with him, even though she liked him so much, and to Pippa it was vitally important to love the man you married.

He had said he understood, accepted that, but he believed she would begin to love him once she was his wife, once they shared their lives fully, and maybe she would. She hoped so.

The car put on more speed. They were coming closer to the little cottage where Pippa lived. Tom came very fast round the final corner just as another car came out of a narrow lane to the right.

Pippa gasped, sitting upright, as tyres screamed on the road surface. Tom put on his brakes and tried to spin the wheel to avoid the other car, but it was too late. The cars hit each other with a violence that threw Pippa forward; she would have gone through the windscreen if her seat belt had not held, and if the airbag had not ballooned outward to cushion her fall.

For a moment or so she was too shocked to move or think, could not remember what had happened. Then she dazedly began to fight her way out of the billowing folds of the airbag, to sit up and take stock. At her side, Tom had also been cushioned by his own airbag, but he had already recovered enough to undo his seat belt and open the car door.

'Are you okay?' she shakily asked him.

'I think so. Stay here,' he muttered.

The other car, a long red sports car, was skewed across the road, its nose buried in the hedge.

Had the driver been killed? she anxiously wondered, as Tom began unsteadily to walk towards it, but then the sports car's door opened and the driver emerged, a tall, lean man, whose immaculate evening dress seemed incongruous in this situation.

Pippa stared, her body pulsing with shock, her heart beating too fast inside her ribcage, her skin cold, her limbs trembling.

The two men faced each other, inches apart. 'Are you hurt?' Tom asked.

A deep voice answered curtly. 'Just cuts and bruises. No thanks to you. What the hell were you doing, driving at that speed?'

Defensively, Tom countered, 'Why did you pull out like that, without looking?'

'I stopped to make the turn. When I looked left the road was empty. I started to come out, then you appeared at about seventy miles an hour. I had no chance to avoid you.'

It was true. Tom had been driving too fast; he should have slowed as he approached the junction. That was what he normally did, but at this time of night he hadn't been expecting to see another vehicle turning out. It was pure luck that the accident hadn't had worse consequences. They could all have been killed.

Tom didn't argue; no doubt he realised he wasn't entirely blameless. He was usually such a careful driver; it wasn't in character for him to take risks.

Glancing past the other man at his red car, he asked, 'Is there much damage to your car?'

They stood with their backs to Pippa, who huddled down inside her black velvet evening jacket, shivering, but not taking her eyes from them. Tom bent down to peer at the sports car's long, sleek bonnet.

'I'm afraid there are a lot of scratches on here.'

'Yes,' the other man agreed angrily. 'It will cost the earth to have the paintwork renewed and the car is new. What about your car? Is that badly damaged?'

He was over six foot, with a long, supple back and even longer legs. As he half turned to glance back at Tom's car she saw his strong features: hard, sardonic, an imperious nose, a generously cut mouth, heavy-lidded eyes, and the way his dark hair curled behind his ears.

He glanced at Tom's car. 'I see you have a passenger,' he murmured. 'An eye witness. A woman? I hope she'll tell the truth if we have to go to court.'

'Don't be offensive,' Tom snapped. 'I admit, I was driving too fast, but I was on the main road. You were coming out of a small lane; you should have waited, let me go past. I'll pay your garage bills; there will be no need to involve the police, or go to court. But if we did my fiancée would tell the absolute truth; I wouldn't ask her to lie.'

The other laughed curtly, his manner making it plain that he did not believe that.

Tom was bristling. Pippa saw his hands screw into fists, but he kept his voice level. 'We had better exchange addresses and the names of our insurance companies. By the way, I work for mine, so you need have no fear they won't pay.'

He turned away to walk back towards his own car. 'I'll get my documents.'

The other man leaned into the red sports car and emerged again with some papers in his hand. He began to follow Tom and Pippa turned her head away, face hidden by the high collar of her velvet jacket.

She sensed the other driver bending to stare at her and closed her eyes, hoping he couldn't see her clearly.

'Is your companion hurt?' he asked Tom, who was

looking into his glove compartment for his documents.

'What?' Tom looked at her. 'Are you okay, Pippa?'

'Just tired,' she whispered huskily, not turning or lifting her head.

But she still felt the probe of the other man's grey eyes and her heart beat like a metronome.

'I'll get you home as soon as I can, darling,' Tom murmured, brushing a strand of her rich chestnut hair back from her forehead.

He turned towards the other driver, proffering the documents he held. The two of them used the bonnet of Tom's car to write down the information each needed. Still keeping her eyes almost closed, Pippa watched through her lashes, breathing unsteadily, hearing the deep, cool voice talking, hoping he wouldn't ask for her address or demand she speak to him.

If she could only get away, escape; she felt doom threaten her, a fate she was not strong enough to withstand. Hurry up, Tom, she thought. Don't stand there talking.

She knew that soothing voice he was using; he was trying to calm the other driver, placate him, talk him round. It was a technique Tom used in business every day; he was an expert at persuading people to do what he wanted.

They worked for an insurance company in central London. Tom was one of the executives who dealt with large claims. He needed all his tact, diplomacy, cool patience, to negotiate with claimants and lawyers. He was doing that now.

Stop talking, Tom, she thought desperately. Get

back in the car and let's drive away. Take me home.
Take me safely home.

The two men shook hands—a typically polite
English gesture. They had come to an agreement.

'Goodnight, Mr Harding. I'll be in touch.'

The other murmured a reply, less clearly, shot another look into the car. Pippa tensed in dread, but he
turned to walk away and she could relax a little, letting out her held breath. He was going.

Tom got back into the car beside her, groaning.

'Well, that was bad luck. My own stupid fault,
driving too fast.' He started the engine; it flared,
raced, while he listened to it anxiously. 'Let's hope
there isn't too much damage.'

'Did you notice much?'

'One wing has crumpled, that will have to be re-
placed, and my door is badly scratched, but it could
have been worse.'

'We could have been killed,' she agreed, her eyes
fixed on the man sliding his long legs back into the
red sports car. The night wind lifted his thick, silky
black hair, winnowing it like caressing fingers.

Yes, it could have been much worse; it could have
been disastrous. Her entire body was limp, as if she
had barely escaped with her life. All the adrenalin had
drained out of her. She yearned to be alone, in her
cottage, to think, to recover from this.

Tom parked outside her cottage a few moments
later and turned to kiss her. 'Goodnight, darling. I'm
sorry about the accident.' He looked down at her,
frowning. 'You're very quiet—are you angry with
me?'

'No, of course not. I'm very tired, that's all.'

'And having an accident didn't help,' he wryly

said, grimacing. 'Sleep well, anyway. I'll see you on Monday.'

She got out of the car, waved to him as he drove off, and let herself into her cottage, switching on the light. Before she could shut the door again a furry black shape brushed past her and ran gracefully through the hall into the kitchen.

Groaning, she closed the door and followed. 'You're a nuisance, you stupid cat. I want to go to bed, not hang around here feeding you.'

Samson ignored her, nose in the air, his elegant black body seated pointedly beside the fridge. He knew there were the remains of a chicken in there, left over from the dinner she had cooked for Tom last night, and although he would eat tinned cat food if nothing else was available his favourite food was roast chicken.

Pippa knew she would get no peace until she had given in, so she got out the chicken and sliced some into Samson's bowl, added crushed biscuit, poured fresh water into another bowl, and put them down. The cat immediately started eating.

Pippa left the kitchen, turning off the light, and went upstairs, stripped, put on a brief green cotton nightdress. In the bathroom she cleaned off her make-up and washed. In the mirror her face was oddly grey, her eyes dilated, black pupils glowing like strange fruit.

Shock, she thought, looking away hurriedly. Returning to her bedroom, she got between the sheets and switched off the light.

The cottage only had two bedrooms and a bathroom; downstairs there was a comfortable sitting room and the kitchen, with its small dining nook at one end. Her firm had helped her with the purchase; the price had been very low because the place had needed so much work. It had been occupied for years by an eccentric old man.

He had left the cottage more or less as it had been when he'd inherited it from his father forty years earlier, she'd been told by the estate agent. He had done no repairs, no redecoration. By the time he died himself, the place had been in a parlous state. But—the agent had beamed—it wouldn't take much trouble to modernise.

She should never have believed him. Even though the price had been low, the mortgage was more than she would have wished to pay. She had very little left over once she had paid it each month. Despite that, she loved this little house; it was the first real home she had ever had.

In her childhood she had passed from one "family" to another. Some foster mothers had only liked small children and hadn't been able to cope with older girls. Once her foster family had split up in divorce and she had been parcelled off to another one. She had yearned for stability, for a sense of belonging, a real home—and at last she had one. No price could be too high for that.

She could do without expensive clothes, make-up, visits to beauty parlours, holidays abroad. She had a home of her own; that was all that mattered.

She had had to minimise the expense of conversion, though. So she had done all the redecorating herself, even painted the outside walls, standing on a rather rickety ladder she had bought for a song in an auction, but she had had to pay a local builder to repair the roof and instal a new bathroom. Those jobs were beyond her.

But when she and Tom were married they would be living here; she wouldn't have to move again. Tom had grown to dislike his own house; living on a housing estate meant living with noisy children running around all day, kicking balls, shouting, riding far too fast on their bicycles along pavements, and his neighbours played their radios and televisions too loudly.

Life would be easier for them if they lived in her cottage. Tom insisted on taking over her mortgage and she meant to pay for all the food they bought. Their joint income would be comfortable. They would even take holidays in the sun in exotic places.

Lying in the dark, staring up at the ceiling, Pippa smiled at that thought. She hadn't been abroad much; she was dying to go to foreign places, enjoy better weather.

An image flashed through her mind with a strangely vivid sensation, as if it was happening now, right now, and she started, shuddering.

The car crash, those terrifying sounds of tyres screaming on tarmac, the airbag ballooning into her face, the red sports car skewed into the hawthorn hedge, the moment when the driver got out.

Her heart beat painfully, her ears drumming with agitated blood. She shut her eyes. She wouldn't think about it. She had to forget; she must clear her head.

Oh, why had it happened? Why now? Fate had a strange sense of humour. Only one more week and she would be Tom's wife. Why had they had the accident, crashed into the man's car, at this particular time?

She tried to sleep, but was awake most of the night.

The flashback kept coming. Her brain was her enemy and would not let her forget. As the hours wore on, her head began to ache. She was first hot, then cold, twisting and turning in the bed, hearing the tick-tick of the clock on her bedside table as though it beat in her blood.

Eventually she did fall into a heavy, stupefied sleep from which she woke abruptly when her alarm went off at nine o'clock. She felt like death as she stumbled out of bed.

After a shower she dressed in jeans and a clean white T-shirt, then went downstairs to make coffee.

Samson gave her an angry greeting. She was usually up well before this time, and like all cats he had a good sense of the time, especially where meals were concerned. While she moved about he kept brushing against her, slithering between her legs, making his demand calls. Miaow. Miaow. Where's my breakfast? Where's my food?

After giving him a saucer of milk and cereal, she let him out of the back door, watched him streak through the little garden, then she poured herself orange juice and sat down to sip it. After contemplating the idea of some toast, she decided against it—she really wasn't hungry.

The dressmaker arrived half an hour later, bright and cheerful in a neat grey skirt and blue blouse. 'Lovely morning, isn't it?' She said as Pippa opened the front door.

'Lovely.' In fact Pippa hadn't noticed; she had been too preoccupied. Now she glanced around, absorbing the bright spring sunshine, the blue sky, the tassels of catkins on a hazel tree in her garden, the frilly yellow daffodils and deep purplish blue of hyacinth. She had planted them last year; this year they had come up without her help.

'Yes, lovely,' she agreed. Another one of Fate's little jokes, this wonderful weather, the beauty of the morning. It should have been stormy, threatening, not full of light and hope. The weather did not fit her mood at all. 'Can I get you some coffee, Mrs Lucas?' she asked, stepping back to let the dressmaker into the hall.

'Thanks, I'd love some later, but I'd like to get on with the fitting first; I have a busy day ahead.' Mrs Lucas considered her, frowning. 'Aren't you well, dear? You're very pale.'

'We went to a party last night, and on the way home we had a bit of an accident.'

'No! Was it serious? Anyone hurt?'

'Thank heavens, no, and the car wasn't badly damaged, but it was a shock.'

'Of course it was. Bound to be. No wonder you're pale. Well, I won't take up too much of your time. There isn't much to do; the dress is nearly finished. I just want to check that it fits perfectly. Have you got everything else, now?'

'Almost everything.'

'Good girl. Well, get your jeans and T-shirt off, stand on that chair, and I'll slip the dress over your head.' Mrs Lucas stood waiting while Pippa obeyed her. The silk and lace dress was carefully held between her two hands and once Pippa was in position she delicately lifted her hands and the dress dropped over Pippa's head and rustled softly as it fell to her feet. There was a small mirror on the wall opposite her; Pippa could see a partial reflection of herself, looking strange and unfamiliar in that dream dress. What was it about a bride that left a romantic glow?

Mrs Lucas got busy with pins, tucking in her waist a fraction, clicking her tongue. 'You've lost weight again! Another pound, I'd say.'

'Sorry. I'm not dieting, honestly. I can't think why I'm losing weight.'

'Oh, it often happens to brides. Wedding nerves, rushing around, forgetting to eat; they always seem to lose weight. Don't worry, I can cope.'

Her mouth full of pins, she adjusted the set of the lacy bodice from which Pippa's head rose so vividly, with that frame of bright chestnut hair lit by morning sunlight. Pippa watched her mirrored image with uneasy green eyes. Everything seemed surreal, unlikely—was that really her?

And if she seemed strange to herself now, she was going to feel much stranger in a week, after her wedding.

Looking at her watch with a groan, Mrs Lucas got up from her knees. 'I must go; I've got so much to do today. I'll just take the dress off, Pippa, before you get down. Next time you see it, it will fit you perfectly, I promise. You're going to be a lovely bride.'

The silk and lace softly, sibilantly, lifted over her head. Mrs Lucas inserted the dress back onto a hanger inside the plastic carrier in which she had brought it, and zipped up the carrier.

'Have you got time for that coffee?'

'Sorry, no, not really. See you soon.'

She was gone a moment later. Pippa put her clothes back on and made herself black coffee, sat sipping it, trying to shake off her disturbed and uneasy mood.

In a week's time...just a week now...she would be

Tom's wife. She should be radiant, over the moon. A woman's wedding day was supposed to be the happiest of her life—so why didn't she feel happy?

Maybe all brides felt this sense of doom, the fear, the sinking in the pit of the stomach close to nausea? Far from being happy, she had a strong feeling that she was about to make the worst mistake of her life.

She must stop thinking like that! What was the matter with her? She was going to be happy. She wouldn't let herself think negative thoughts.

She went to bed early that evening and was up in good time to get to work. Tom was always there early, and expected her to be early too. Working in an insurance company wasn't exactly thrilling, but the job paid well and the work was never complicated or difficult.

Monday was always a calm day; the postbag was light and their workload was easy enough to deal with as they always tried to clear their desks by Friday afternoon, so she was able to go to lunch a little early that day, to give herself time to get to Bond Street, and then hopefully grab a snack before she went back to the office.

She caught a bus, then walked anxiously, hurriedly, to the bridal shop, relieved to see that the pearl and rose coronet was still in the window. The assistant sat her in a chair in front of a mirror, brought a wedding veil and the coronet for her to try on.

Pippa gazed at herself, smiling; it really was perfect, just what she wanted.

'You look lovely,' the assistant told her, and Pippa thought she looked pretty good, too.

'It's exactly what I've been looking for,' she confessed. 'I'll take it.'

Then the smile went and her eyes widened in horror as she saw a reflection of the street outside behind her shoulders.

A man stood there, staring at her: tall, elegantly dressed, his black hair brushed and immaculate.

In the mirror their eyes met. His were fixed and glittering, bright and hot as burning stars. Pippa stared into them, her stomach turning over, grew icy cold and fainted.

CHAPTER TWO

SHE recovered consciousness slowly, not quite sure what had happened, her lids flickering, then rising; she looked up, her green eyes dazed, not focusing properly.

Two faces bent over her. The assistant looked anxious, upset. The other...

Pippa took one look at him and promptly shut her eyes again. She did not want to believe he was real. Surely she wasn't imagining things, dreaming him up in the oddest places, at the oddest times? Her head buzzed with distressed questions. What was he doing here? Come to that, what had he been doing outside the bridal shop? What was going on? First the accident; now he'd turned up while she was trying on her bridal coronet. What was Fate up to?

'She's fainted again,' the assistant said. 'Oh, dear. Do you think she's really ill? She's very pale. Should I ring for an ambulance? Or a doctor?'

'No, I don't think she's ill; she's just playing dead,' said the deep, cool voice she remembered so well.

How dared he? What right did he have to read her so accurately? Angrily she opened her eyes once more and glared at him, beginning to get up.

It didn't make her any less furious that he helped, as effortlessly as if she weighed no more than a child, lifting her with one arm around her waist, his warm hand just below her breast, the intimacy of the contact making her heart thud painfully.

'Oh...perhaps we shouldn't move her yet,' the assistant nervously murmured. 'She may still be groggy.'

'Oh, she'll be okay. Would you run out and stop that taxi going past? Thanks.'

Pippa was still being held close to that long, lean body; the proximity was doing drastic things to her, especially when she looked up and sideways at the hard-edged, smooth-skinned, masculine face.

She heard the other girl's high heels clipping across the shop and knew she was alone with him. Panic streaked through her; she pushed him away and his arm dropped.

Those bright eyes gleamed with what she grimly recognised as mockery. So he was finding the situation funny, was he? Her teeth met.

'Feeling better now?' he enquired softly.

'Yes, thank you.' Her voice was cold and remote, hiding the rage she felt although she suspected he wasn't missing it; his argument was open, unhidden.

The shop assistant rushed back, breathlessly said, 'The taxi's waiting.'

'Thank you.' He looked at Pippa. 'Maybe you should take the veil off before we go?'

'We' go? she thought. She wasn't going anywhere with him.

But the assistant came to help her. 'So, did you want the coronet?'

'Yes, please.' Pippa fumbled in her bag, found her credit card and held it out.

The assistant offered her the payment slip a moment later and she signed it, then took back her card and put it away, very slowly and carefully, deliberately delaying in the hope that he might go outside to talk to the taxi driver.

She might then have a chance to escape, run off down the road, but he waited beside her, perhaps anticipating her intention. Finally she had to leave the shop, as they walked out on to the pavement he held her elbow lightly, propelled her towards the taxi.

'I don't want to...' she breathed.

'You might faint again; we can't have that.' He smiled, lifting her into the back of the taxi.

She couldn't quite catch what he said to the driver before climbing in beside her, but before she could ask him the taxi set off with a jerk which almost made her tumble forward on to the floor.

'Do up your seat belt,' she was ordered, and her companion leaned over to drag the belt across her shoulder and down to her waist, clip it into place, his long fingers brushing her thigh. He had a fresh, outdoor scent: pine, she decided, inhaling it. She wished he would stop invading her body space. It was far too disturbing.

'Where did you tell the driver to go?' she asked huskily as he sat back, not meeting the eyes that watched her as if he could read her every thought.

'I feel it's time we had a private chat. I told him to take us to my hotel. Have you had lunch?'

Agitated, she protested, 'I'm not going to your hotel! I have to get back to work.'

'You can ring and tell them you've been taken ill,' he dismissed. 'Have you had lunch?'

'Yes,' she lied, and received one of his dry, mocking glances.

'Where? You came out of your office, caught a bus

and went straight to that shop. Where could you have had lunch?'

'You've been following me? Spying on me? How dare you? You had no right,' she spluttered, very flushed now. 'Were you on the bus? I didn't see you.'

'No, I followed in a taxi, then walked behind you along Bond Street.'

She thought harder, forehead wrinkled. 'How did you know where I worked?'

'Your fiancé told me where he worked, so I rang up and asked the switchboard if you worked there, too.'

Simple when you know how, she thought; she should have guessed he would track her down if he wanted to, but she hadn't thought he would want to.

'They tried to put me through, but someone in your office said you had just left, were going shopping in your lunch hour. I was ringing on my mobile from the foyer of the building. A minute later I saw you come out of the lift so I followed.'

She was speechless. He made it sound perfectly normal to follow people around, spy on them—nothing to get excited about. But she was so furious she couldn't even get a word out.

He gave her a wry grin, eyes teasing. 'Stop glaring at me. I had to see you. You knew that, from the minute his car crashed into mine. You knew we had to meet again, that we have a lot to talk about.'

'We have nothing to talk about! I don't want to talk to you at all. I just want to get back to my office and forget you exist.'

But she was so nervous that she put up a shaky hand to brush stray strands of bright hair away from her cheek, aware that he watched the tiny movement with those intent, glittering eyes.

'And you think you can do that, Pippa?' he drawled, moving even closer so that their bodies touched.

She couldn't bear the contact, shifted away into the corner, body tense and shuddering.

'Yes.' But her eyes didn't meet his and she felt him staring at the telltale pulse beating hard in her throat.

He reached out a hand; one long finger slid down her cheek then down her neck, awaking pulses everywhere it rested, until it pressed down into that pulse in her throat. 'What's the point of lying? You're not convincing me; you're only lying to yourself.'

'Don't touch me!' she muttered, knocking his hand away.

The taxi turned into a hotel entrance, set back from the road. She looked up at the grand façade, ornate and baroque, with ironwork balconies outside every other widow, flags flying on the steep roof. She had heard of the hotel but never been inside it; it was far too expensive. Normally she would have loved to go there for lunch, but not with him.

'You get out here; I'll go on to my office!' she insisted, holding on to the seat with both hands.

To her relief and surprise, he got out without replying and paid the driver. Only then did he turn back towards Pippa. 'Out you get!' He reached over and undid her seat belt before she had notice of his intention.

She wanted to yell, scream, hit him, but the hotel doorman had appeared behind him, magnificent in livery dripping with gold braid, smiling an obsequious welcome, and she was too embarrassed to make a scene in front of such an audience.

'I can't. Let me go,' she said instead, very quietly, still hanging on to the seat.

'Let me help you,' he blandly murmured, and the next second he had taken her by the waist and was lifting her out of the taxi. Keeping his arm around her, he guided her up the steps into the hotel foyer while the doorman closed the taxi door and followed them. A moment later Pippa found herself being propelled into a lift; the door shut and the lift began to rise.

There was nobody else in the lift with them; she felt free to break away from him, using every ounce of her strength, looking at him with angry hostility as she reeled against the lift wall.

'How dare you manhandle me like this? And if you think you can get me up to your bedroom...'

'Suite,' he coolly corrected. 'There's a sitting room; we can have lunch there.'

'I am not going with you! Bedroom or suite, I am not going anywhere alone with you!'

'You're alone with me now,' he pointed out in silky tones, leaning over her in what she interpreted as menace, despite the laughter gleaming in his eyes. His proximity was threat enough, even when he didn't touch her.

'Stop it! Keep away from me!' she whispered, trembling.

His face was inches away from her own. 'What are you so afraid of, Pippa? Me? Or yourself?'

Confused, she muttered, 'Don't be stupid. How can I be afraid of myself?'

'Of what you really want,' he enlarged, eyes watching her intently. 'Of your own instinct and desires. You're so terrified of how you feel that you need to shelter behind a pretence of hating me. You can't risk so much as a look at me, can you?'

Face burning, eyes flickering nervously, she said, 'I don't know what you're talking about. Do I have to remind you that I'm getting married in a week's time?'

The lift stopped and the doors opened. Nobody was waiting on that floor; there was no one in view at all. He stepped out, grabbed her hand and jerked her out after him.

'I am not going with you! Let go of me!' She struggled to get away, flailing at him with one hand, managed to land a blow on his cheek, and gave a little cry of pain as she hurt herself on the hard edge of his bone structure.

'Serves you right! You shouldn't be so violent!' He ran an exploring hand over his cheek where a red mark burnt. 'That hurt me almost as much as it probably hurt you.'

'Good!'

A room door nearby opened and an old lady in a pink linen suit, wearing a small black hat with a black lace veil which fell over her eyes, came out, gave them a startled, uneasy look.

'Is anything wrong?' she quavered.

Pippa hesitated fatally; he answered before she could. 'She's shy, that's all. Honeymoon nerves! You know how women get on these occasions.'

The old lady blushed and then smiled; Pippa glared at him. He was maddening; he always had been.

'I should carry you over the threshold, darling,' he said, and suddenly grabbed Pippa off her feet before she could stop him, lifted her up into his arms and strode off with her while the old lady gazed after them with a romantic smile.

Pippa knew she should call his bluff, struggle, hit him again, but with that happy, wide-eyed audience she simply couldn't. In any case a moment later he paused in front of double doors, produced a key and unlocked the suite, carried Pippa inside, into a small hallway, and closed the door behind them with his elbow.

'Put me down!' she hoarsely demanded. 'Put me down at once!'

He carried her into a bedroom and dropped her on the large, white-and silver-draped bed.

Her heart beat wildly in her throat. Surely he didn't intend... She rolled over to the far edge of the bed and shakily stood up, looking around for a weapon to use if he tried to come anywhere near her. The table lamp looked heavy; it had a bronze cast base and could probably kill someone.

But he was turning back towards the door. Over his shoulder he casually said, 'Use the bathroom, if you wish. Your hair could certainly do with some attention.'

The door closed behind him. She was alone and safe, for the moment. Her gaze wandered round the room, absorbing the luxury of the furnishings: high French windows covered with lace and floor-length curtains that matched the white and silver satin bed-cover, the bronze-based lamps with their wide silver satin shades, walnut-veneered furniture that was prob-ably reproduction, not genuinely antique, a chest, a wardrobe whose doors were set with mirrors, a dressing table on which stood a vase of white carnations and roses.

She began to walk towards the door of the *en-suite* bathroom, paused to bend over the flowers, inhaling their faint scent then hurried on, in case he came back.

The bathroom was entirely white, with nineteen-twenties-style fittings, elegant fluted chrome taps. In a cupboard above the vanity unit she found his toiletries: aftershave, an electric razor, shower gel, shampoo. Somehow it was too intimate to stare at them. She quickly shut the door on them and opened her bag.

She found a comb and ran it through her hair, renewed her make up, considered her reflection, disturbed by the feverish brightness of her eyes, the faint tremble of her mouth, the fast beating of that pulse in her neck.

It was crazy to let him do this to her. She had to pull herself together and somehow talk her way out of this suite. She had given him time to calm down, to think—maybe now he would realise he had to let her leave?

Turning away, she picked up her bag and left the bathroom, quietly opened the door of the bedroom. If he wasn't in earshot she might be able to get away now.

She couldn't hear a sound so she began tiptoeing back along the little hall towards the outer door. Before she reached it, however, a voice spoke softly behind her.

'Don't even think about it.'

She froze, looking round.

He was leaning on the open doorway into what she glimpsed to be a sitting room, his arms crossed, his body lounging with casual grace, those long legs relaxed, making her forcibly aware of his intense sexual allure, the gleaming display of the peacock. And he knew it, too; he was watching her with that infuriating mockery, knowing what she was feeling, amused and sure of himself.

She probably still had time to make a run for it, but he would only take a few seconds to catch up with her and her self-respect wouldn't allow her to make a fight of this. In any case, she knew she would only lose. She had to use other weapons against him.

'I have to get back to work.'

'I've already rung your office and told them you fainted and would be going home to rest instead of going to work.'

She furiously broke out, 'You had no business to do that!'

He ignored her angry splutter. 'I've ordered lunch, too—something simple. I thought you wouldn't want anything elaborate. Salad, some cheese, cold beef and chicken, some wholemeal bread, pickles, some fruit, yogurt, and a pot of coffee.'

'I'm not hungry. You eat lunch; I'll get back to my office.' She turned towards the door of the suite.

'Do I have to carry you in here?' his voice silkily enquired, and she froze.

'Why are you doing this?' she burst out. 'What's the point? You're married; I'm getting married—we have nothing to say to each other.'

Four years ago she had joined his firm after the company she had been working for had gone into liquidation. Pippa had been shocked by the news that everyone was being made redundant, but by sheer good luck she had got a new job the same day. During her lunch hour she had gone into an employment agency to register and had been given an immediate interview with a nearby office.

She had walked down the road, very nervous, a little shaky, and been shown up to the personnel officer, who had tested her various secretarial skills and spent half an hour questioning her.

Pippa hadn't expected to be given a job there and then, but the personnel officer had leaned back at last and said, 'When can you start?'

Heart lifting, Pippa whispered, 'Do you mean I've got a job here? You're taking me on?'

The woman smiled, eyes amused. 'That's what I mean. So when can you start?'

She didn't need to think about it; she knew she would be out of a job by the end of that week and would need to be earning again as soon as possible. She had no one to help her with her rent and the cost of living. She only had herself to rely on.

'On Monday?' Relief and delight were filling her.

'Wonderful. Report to me at nine o'clock and I'll have someone show you to your desk. You'll be working in the managing director's office. His private assistant will be in charge; she'll tell you what she wants you to do. It isn't a difficult job, but it's vital that everything runs smoothly in that office and Miss Dalton is a tough organiser. Be careful not to annoy her. The MD insists on a smooth-running office.'

It sounded rather nerve-racking to Pippa, but the salary was good and the work not too onerous. She left there walking on air, and got back to find everyone else in her office gloomily contemplating living on social security until they found work elsewhere.

'What about you, Pippa?' asked the girl whose desk was opposite hers. 'What will you do?'

'Oh, I've got a new job. I start there next Monday,' Pippa airily told her, and everyone else stared in disbelief.

'How on earth did you manage that?'

'Just luck.' She told them what had happened and they were envious and incredulous.

'I'm going there as soon as I've finished work,' one of them said, and others nodded their heads.

By the end of the week at least half of them had managed to find new jobs—some just about adequate, although one of them had got a much better job. There was a much more cheerful atmosphere in the office. They had a big party in a local Chinese restaurant on the Friday evening, knowing that they would probably not see each other again, although some close friends would keep in touch. Working together was a matter of propinquity. Once they all split up their friendships would begin to fade.

It had been Pippa's first job. She had only been sixteen when she started work there and now she was twenty but felt older because ever since she'd left her last foster home she had been living alone, in one room, managing a tight budget, always struggling to make ends meet. That had made her grow up fast, had taught her a discipline she relied on to help her through each day. She couldn't allow herself to buy anything she could do without; thrift was essential on such a small amount of money.

Her clothes had to last and look good in the office so she bought inexpensive but well-made skirts and blouses which she could vary daily, and wash again and again. She ate little, bought cheaply in street markets, mostly vegetables and fruit, pasta, some fish now and again, or more rarely, chicken. She only had one electric ring to cook on; she had to choose easily cooked food.

She had never been able to afford to entertain so she didn't accept invitations from other people, since she couldn't reciprocate. Once or twice she had had a date with one of the young men in the office, but none of them had attracted her much and the dates had been rather dull.

She felt a little sad, saying goodbye to people she had worked with for four years, though. She was going to miss them. All the same, she was deeply relieved to have another job to go to immediately. She couldn't imagine how she would have paid the rent otherwise. The life of the street people, homeless and hopeless, gave her nightmares for a while. Being made redundant like that had destabilised her life, made her feel threatened, even after she'd got that new job.

On the following Monday she nervously made her way to the office block where she would be working, was taken up in the lift from the personnel office by one of the girls who worked there.

'You know who you'll be working for? Mr Harding, the managing director.' Her voice had a reverent note. 'You're so lucky. He's gorgeous. And nice. But he's married, worse luck! His wife is really lovely; she's a model. You often see her in glossy magazines. They make a stunning couple.'

'What exactly will my job entail?' Pippa asked. 'I was never told.' That was what interested her, not the sexiness or availability of the boss.

The other girl shrugged. 'Working on a word processor, sending out letters, sorting mail, taking phone calls—the usual office routine. There are half a dozen girls working in the office and Mr Harding's PA is a dragon lady. Miss Dalton.'

'The personnel officer warned me to be very careful with her.'

'She wasn't kidding. She bites!'

She hadn't exaggerated, Pippa discovered a few minutes later, contemplating the tall, cold-eyed woman who ran the office.

Felicity Dalton wasn't beautiful, but she was striking—very thin and elegant, with long, straight black hair she wore drawn off her face and held with a large black clip. In her beautifully shaped ears she wore diamond studs. Her white blouse was immaculate, her black jersey skirt emphasised the sleek lines of her body. She looked as if she had been sculpted out of ice. A snow queen who clearly did not like people much, especially those of her own sex, whom she treated with hostility and contempt.

She gave Pippa brusque instructions, left her seated at a desk and went back to her own private office.

The other girls all grinned at Pippa once Felicity Dalton had gone. 'Scary, isn't she?' one whispered. 'I'm Judy, by the way.'

She was the same age as Pippa, and immediately likeable, a short, rather plump girl with curly brown hair and bright brown eyes, the pupils circled by golden rays which made her look like a lion.

'Hi. I'm Pippa.'

'Lovely name. Mine's so ordinary.' Judy sighed, then went on, 'If you need any help, just ask. It's not so long since I was new here; I know how it feels.'

Over that first week Pippa had to go to Judy for

help more than once. Some of the letters they had to send were automatic replies to particular types of complaint; she wasn't always sure which reply to send but Judy knew the office routine by heart.

The managing director himself was away, Pippa discovered, so their workload was not as heavy as it would be when he was working there.

'What's he like?' she asked Judy, whose brown-gold eyes turned dreamy.

'Very sexy. The Dalton's crazy about him, but she'll never get anywhere. He's married to a really stunning woman; he never notices the Dalton at all. That's what burns her up, why she's so frozen and nasty. She's hurting, so she makes sure we all feel the same.'

'Poor Miss Dalton,' Pippa said, with the first real sympathy she had felt for the older woman, who was never pleasant to her.

'Don't feel sorry for her! Just because her heart's breaking is no reason why she should make our lives hell, is it?' Judy was made of sterner stuff; her brown eyes glinted crossly.

Pippa grinned at her. 'No reason at all, no! Anyway, you didn't say what he was like to work for!'

'He's quite tough, too, actually, but in a different way. He expects us to work very hard, and he won't tolerate mistakes, but he isn't nasty, like Dalton. So long as you work hard he's decent to you. Half the girls in the office are nuts about him, but he never encourages them. He's a happily married man.'

'Has he got children?'

'One, a boy, around four years old, called Johnny. Randal has a big silver-framed photo of him on his desk. And another photo of his wife in evening dress—she really is fantastic. Wait until you see her!'

She was not to see Mrs Harding for some months, but Randal Harding was back at work the following Monday. Pippa had got in early to give herself a head start; she was only just able to keep up with the work as yet, and Miss Dalton was watching her like a hawk, pouncing on her every mistake. Pippa could not afford to lose this job, so she'd got an earlier bus that morning.

It was a fresh, blustery day; her curly chestnut hair had got blown about as she'd walked along the road, and her skin was flushed with exercise and cool air.

Nobody else was in her office; she sat down in front of her word processor and switched on, arranged her pens beside a pad next to the phone and was about to start work when the door opened. Looking round with a smile, Pippa was startled to see a man entering the office. She got an immediate impression of height and dark, brooding good looks.

He looked surprised too, staring at her. 'Who are you?'

She didn't like his curt tone. Coldly, she answered, 'I work here. Who are you?'

'I'm the managing director.'

She gulped. Oh, no! She should have guessed. She had known he would be back at work today.

'Would you make me some coffee and bring it through to my office?' he asked. 'Bring a pad, too. I want you to take dictation.'

The door shut again; he was gone, leaving Pippa breathless. Well, that hadn't been a good beginning, had it? She wouldn't have left a very favourable impression on *him*. And she had been so keen to impress him!

Hurriedly she made him coffee, got a few biscuits from the tin kept in the cupboard where the coffee-making equipment was stored, laid a tray, collected her pad and several pens, and went through to his office.

That first session with Randal was tense and anxious; she was terrified of making a mistake. He was clearly in a temper; she sensed he would have gone into hyper-rage for any reason, however slight. So she concentrated hard, listening intently, her pen moving fast and fluently over the pad while he dictated several memos to staff, letters to clients.

Miss Dalton arrived just as he finished. Pippa incredulously saw that the snow queen looked flustered, her skin flushed, apologising as she hurried into the room, still wearing her smart black raincoat.

'I am so sorry, Mr Harding; I left early so that I would be here when you arrived, but there was some sort of hold-up on the buses; I had to wait for ages before I could get one.'

He nodded impatiently. 'Never mind, Miss Dalton. Pippa was here early and has taken dictation.' He looked at Pippa. 'Get those ready to sign as soon as possible, would you? Thank you.'

Pippa retreated, still shaky, and felt Miss Dalton's icy eyes on her all the way.

Judy was just hanging up her coat. 'Where have you been?' she asked, and Pippa told her in a whisper. Judy whistled. 'She won't forgive you for that for a long time! The boss is her property; she'll hate you for being here when she wasn't.'

She was absolutely right. Miss Dalton was on

Pippa's case all day, snapping at her, complaining about her work, criticising her for wearing eye make-up, not to mention vivid red varnish on her fingernails in the office.

'You look like a tart! Mr Harding doesn't like his employees to wear that much make-up! Don't come to work like that again!'

Pippa mumbled an apology; the other girls discreetly averted their heads.

Later that morning Miss Dalton struck again accusing her of gossiping to Judy when she should be working.

'I've finished the work Mr Harding asked me to do—shall I take the letters to him to sign?'

'No,' snapped Miss Dalton. 'I'll do it!' She came over to Pippa's desk, picked up the perfectly typed letters and went out with them.

'Brrr…icy weather,' Judy whispered. 'I told you so. She hates you now. Take another step near Mr Harding and she'll kill you.'

'It isn't fair. He asked me to take dictation, and I did—it wasn't my fault she wasn't here.'

Miss Dalton came briskly back and loaded Pippa with more work, telling her to hurry up and finish it.

All that day, Pippa couldn't do anything right.

It was huge relief when Miss Dalton finally departed, leaving Pippa to finish a new pile of work she had been given to do.

'I'll be here for hours—she wants all this done by the morning,' Pippa moaned once the door had shut on the older woman.'

'That will teach you,' Judy teased before she left. 'In future try not to be seen with the boss! Remember, you are a lowly slave and she is the queen!'

It was another hour before Pippa finally got to the bottom of the pile and could switch off her machine and clear her desk. Everyone else had gone; the offices were empty and silent. As she got up to leave the door opened and to her dismay there was Randal Harding again.

Glancing at him, she felt her heart flip over—he was intensely sexy, in his three-piece dark suit, a smooth-fitting waistcoat over his white shirt. He leaned against the doorframe, re-knotting his maroon silk tie.

'Still here? You work long hours, very conscientious,' he said with a faintly teasing smile. 'Everyone else gone?'

She nodded dumbly, unable to speak because he made her so self-conscious.

'Come on, then; the cleaners will be here in a minute.' He switched off the lights, plunging the room into darkness, and she hurried towards the door, stumbling into him and feeling something like an electric shock at the contact.

'Have you got far to go? Where do you live?' he asked.

'West Hackham. Twenty minutes by bus,' she whispered, keeping her eyes down. She was terrified in case Miss Dalton should still be somewhere around, or heard they had left together. Her life wouldn't be worth living if that happened.

'Same direction as me. I'll give you a lift. My car's parked just down here; come along.'

She hung back, 'No, really, it doesn't matter.'

He gave her a wry, amused look. 'Don't look so scared. I don't bite and I won't make a pass.'

She flushed in horror. 'No, I didn't mean...didn't think...'

He took her elbow and propelled her onwards. 'Do you live at home, or have you got your own place?'

Why was he asking that? she wondered, still pink and uncertain. The other girls hadn't said anything about him making passes. Indeed, they'd said he was happily married. Maybe her imagination was working overtime.

They left the building and turned down into the underground car park. Pippa's eyes widened as they halted beside a long, sleek black Jaguar saloon. She had never driven in a car like that before.

He unlocked the car and put her into the front passenger seat. Pippa stroked the cream leather upholstery, gazed at the polished walnut dashboard, equipped with all sorts of gadgets, including a CD player. It must have cost the earth; he must be very wealthy.

As he started the engine he asked her, 'Where did you work before you joined us, and why did you leave?'

She told him the name of her old firm. 'They went into liquidation. We were all made redundant.'

He gave her a sidelong smile of sympathy. 'Tough luck—were you out of work long before you came to us?'

'No, I only left them the week before I joined you.'

'That must have been a relief; no joke being unemployed. I hope you're going to be happy with us.'

'I'm sure I will be,' she said, suppressing all memory of Miss Dalton. 'I already feel at home in the office.'

He flashed her that warm, sideways smile that

changed his face entirely. 'Good. The work you did for me this morning was excellent. If you keep that standard up, we'll feel we were lucky to get you.'

Out of the corner of her eye she watched his long-fingered hands on the wheel, his dark jacket sleeves shooting back to show his immaculate white shirt cuffs. She couldn't blame Miss Dalton for being crazy about him; it would be easy to get that way. His hard profile had a power and masculinity that would have made a strong impact even if he had not been very good-looking, and now that he was no longer in a temper she began to see a charm and warmth that had not been visible when they'd first met.

She hoped he would be like this most of the time, not in that stormy, brooding state. Why had he come to work in that mood today? Had he had a row with his wife?

He drew up outside her address and shot a look up at the shabby Victorian house, the woodwork cracked and peeling, the front door needing new paint. The garden was neglected and overgrown, full of uncut grass and rambling bushes.

'Is this your family home?' he asked slowly.

'No, it's let out by the room—I rent one room here.'

He grimaced. 'If I were you, I'd move. It looks as if cockroaches and rats live here, too.'

'No cockroaches or rats, but there is the odd mouse,' she admitted. 'I don't like to kill the one in my room; like me, it has to live somewhere! But this place is cheap, and the room is quite spacious. I'm used to it.' And she couldn't afford anywhere better.

'Where do your family live?'

She hesitated, hating to talk about her background, then defiantly told him, 'I haven't got one.'

He shot her a sharp look. 'No parents?' He sounded incredulous, disbelieving.

'No family at all.'

His grey eyes searched her face; she looked away from their penetrating probe, feeling like someone under searchlights.

'How long have you been alone?'

'Always.' She paused, hesitating about saying any more, then plunged on, 'I was found as a baby. I've no idea who I really am or who my mother was.'

There was a little silence, then he said gently, 'I'm sorry. You can't have had a very happy childhood. I'm lucky. I have a sister, although both my parents are dead now. And I'm married, of course, with a child. Having a family roots you in life.'

'Yes,' she muttered, because she, of all people, knew that. She dreamt of marrying one day, having children, having a family of her own at last.

She didn't want to talk to him any more; she hurriedly got out of the car, whispering, 'Thanks for the lift, Mr Harding. Goodnight.'

He sat watching her as she fled up the path and unlocked the front door. Pippa was aware of his gaze, but didn't look back. She was a very down-to-earth person; she knew she must not let herself think about him too much. He was her boss; that was all. Just that, nothing else, ever.

Yet whenever she forgot to keep a guard on her mind she thought about him that evening, sitting in her lonely room, listening to her second-hand radio. She couldn't afford a television but radio was some sort of companion: another voice in her room, music, plays.

She had never been in love, never thought much about other people. Now she couldn't stop thinking about Randal Harding, remembering his vivid grey eyes, the charm of his smile, the grace and beauty of his male body.

She was filled with curiosity about him. Was his home as beautiful as his car? Elegant, luxurious, comfortable? He wouldn't be alone tonight, like her—he would have his wife and child for company. Did he know how lucky he was?

That was the beginning. Over the weeks that followed she saw him most days, and each time he gave her that smile, sending her temperature sky-high. Occasionally she had to work for him, and tried hard to stay calm and collected, but it wasn't easy when it made her heart race dangerously whenever he smiled or his hand brushed hers.

One day he called her into his office while Miss Dalton was having coffee in a café across the street with some friends—a birthday celebration, Judy had told Pippa. Judy knew all the office gossip: what was going on and who was dating who.

'They make these wonderful cakes,' she'd said enviously. 'Coffee-iced walnut cakes, chocolate eclairs that melt in your mouth. It's the place to go, if you can afford it. I've been once and still dream about it.'

'Sounds blissful,' Pippa had agreed; she could never have afforded food like that. Her budget was far too restricted.

Mr Harding had put his head round the door at that minute. 'Come through,' he told Pippa, who had got up, flushed and anxious, while Judy whistled under her breath.

'Let's hope Dalton doesn't get back while you're with him! Or your head will roll. Come to that, I'm suspicious, too—why does he always ask for you? Why never me?'

Pippa hadn't even tired to answer that; she couldn't. Randal had taken some sort of interest in her from the beginning—was it because of what he had found out about her background? Was he sorry for her? She didn't like that idea.

When she went into the other room and found Randal Harding standing with his back to her, staring out of the window at the blue, cloudless sky, she began to breathe rapidly, shallowly. While she gazed at that long, supple back, those even longer legs, he turned his head to smile at her, making her heart roll over in a now familiar, disturbing fashion.

'I want to ask a favour of you—this isn't work, so feel free to refuse if you're not happy about it—but I'm very busy today and I can't spare the time to do it myself. My son is five tomorrow and I haven't bought him a birthday present yet. Do you think you could go shopping and choose something for him?'

Taken aback, since she hadn't expected that request, she stammered, 'Well, of course, but...I don't know what toys he already has or what he likes...'.

'He hasn't got any big vehicles—trucks, farm vehicles, fire engines, that sort of thing. He loves toy cars, so that would probably be the best bet.'

'Right, then; okay, I'll do my best. When did you want me to go?'

'Take an extra hour for lunch.' He pulled out a sheaf of bank notes from a wallet in his jacket, and counted some out into her hand. 'That should be enough. And would you buy a birthday card, too?'

His fingers brushed hers, making her legs turn weak, but she nodded, smiling, and hurriedly retreated.

She managed to do her shopping in a world-famous toyshop. It only took a few minutes to choose and pay for a huge bright red fire engine with expanding ladders and tiny firemen in yellow helmets, coiled water hoses, all the equipment a boy would need to play firemen. In another shop she bought a card which she thought quite funny, with a big gold number five on it and a line of pink elephants dancing and playing the trumpet.

She had lunch nearby, before returning to work at the usual time. Miss Dalton was at lunch when Pippa got back.

'She was looking for you,' Judy warned. 'Asking why you had gone to lunch early and who gave you permission. I played dumb, said I didn't know. Where have you been, anyway?'

'Shopping,' Pippa said, rushing into Randal Harding's office and laying the package she had bought on his desk, then hurrying back before Miss Dalton caught her. The last thing she needed was trouble.

'I worry about you,' Judy said. 'What's going on between you and Randal?'

'Nothing! Don't be silly.' Pippa buried herself in her work.

She got into trouble when Miss Dalton returned ten minutes later and demanded to know why Pippa had gone to lunch early.

'I had some urgent shopping to do,' Pippa said, eyes lowered.

'I don't believe my ears! So you just went off to do it without a word!'

Pippa thought of telling her Randal Harding had given her permission to go, but decided that might merely make matters worse, so said nothing.

'How dare you walk out of here without permission? You will go to lunch at the time allotted to you in future.' Miss Dalton's voice was acid. 'One more trick like that and you're out of a job!'

Pippa shivered. She needed this job; there was no guarantee she would get another. Without an income she would find life very hard. 'I'm sorry,' she whispered.

'You'll be even more sorry if you keep annoying me like this!' the older woman snapped.

Judy rolled her eyes at Pippa behind Miss Dalton's back and mouthed, 'I told you so!'

As the time to stop work came closer Miss Dalton came over to look at Pippa's desk and gave her an icy, triumphant smile.

'You've fallen behind again, I see. Your work is far from satisfactory. Well, I want all those letters finished when I come into work tomorrow—understood?'

'Yes, Miss Dalton,' Pippa wearily said; she seemed to spend her life running on the spot just to keep up. She had never had this trouble before.

When everyone had gone she put her head down on the desk, tears welling up into her eyes. Day after day Miss Dalton attacked her, overloaded her with work, watched her like a hawk, and Pippa was exhausted by the strain of it. She had enjoyed her last job; everyone had been friendly, she had been able to keep up with her work. But now she didn't know if she could keep on going; she might have to resign— was that what Miss Dalton wanted? Was she trying to drive her out?

'What's wrong?'

The voice made her stiffen, instinctively wiping her wet eyes with the back of her hard before she sat up.

'Nothing...sorry...just tired,' she mumbled, avoiding Randal Harding's eyes.

He came over to her desk, put an imperative hand under her chin and tilted her face, stared down at it, his grey eyes moving from her wide, wet green eyes to the tremulous curve of her pink mouth.

'You've been crying.'

'Just tired,' she stupidly repeated, staring up at him, conscious of a now familiar turmoil in her body . Her heart was beating so hard it deafened her; she couldn't breathe properly, couldn't focus on his face, which loomed far too close to her own.

'Nonsense, something else is wrong—tell me!'

She shook her head, her mouth dry and her blood running like fire. Never in her life had she felt like this; it was terrifying. Was she falling in love with him? That would be folly, but she had no idea how to stop herself.

His face seemed to be coming closer all the time. She gazed into those brilliant grey eyes, so dazed and confused she couldn't think straight, then her stare dropped to focus on his hard, male mouth, and panic rushed through her.

Was she imagining it, simply because she hungered for it so much, or was he about to kiss her? A second later his mouth touched hers and she shuddered, eyes closing.

His kiss was light and cool for a second or two, then it took fire and his arms went round her, pulling her up from her chair, dragging her so close to him that she felt the pressure of his thighs, the warmth of his body under his elegant clothes, the fierce beating of his heart.

Pippa had never been kissed, touched, like that before. She didn't know what to do, how to feel. Eyes shut tight, plunged into deep, velvety blackness, she swayed helplessly in his arms, her lips parting to give him access to her mouth, entirely given up to him in unconscious surrender.

Only when he lifted his mouth and broke the spell holding her did she begin to think again, and then shame and shock made her turn first red, then white.

'No, you mustn't! You're married!' she broke out.

He looked down at her, his face a battleground of conflicting feelings, gave a long groan. 'Yes. I'm sorry, I shouldn't have touched you. I didn't intend to kiss you. I just couldn't help it.' He ran a caressing hand down her face, trailed his fingers over her mouth, awakening all her pulses again.

'Don't,' she whispered, dying to have him kiss her again.

'God, if only you weren't so young!' he muttered. 'Practically a child. I have no right to come anywhere near you; don't think I'm not ashamed of myself. I just don't seem able to stop thinking about you. I've been wanting to kiss you for a very long time.'

'Randal,' she moaned, shuddering. 'But we can't...shouldn't... You're married.' A pang of jealousy wrenched her. 'And your wife is beautiful.'

His face hardened, darkened. 'Oh, yes, she's beautiful. But our marriage is a sham. We rarely even see each other. She has been having an affair for a year; she's often away—why do you think I asked you to buy the present for Johnny? My wife isn't at home; she has probably forgotten his birthday.'

Startled and distressed, Pippa said, 'Oh...I'm sorry. Really, very sorry. That's very sad. I thought you were happily married; everyone said so.' Then she bit her lip, frowning, as a new idea came to her. 'But I don't want you to use me to get your own back on your wife, or to boost your ego. I'm not a consolation prize, Mr Harding.'

His mouth twisted bitterly. 'I wasn't using you that way, Pippa. Believe me. I kissed you because the temptation was irresistible, that's all. The minute I saw you I wanted to kiss you. It has nothing to do with my wife. I fell out of love with her long ago. Our marriage is over in everything but name. Her current affair is about the third. They never last long, but while they last they're all she cares about. I haven't divorced her yet because of Johnny. I don't care a damn if I never see her again, but I love my son and I don't want him made unhappy.'

'No, poor little boy. He must miss his mother when she's away,' Pippa said, sighing. 'My childhood was pretty grim. I'd have given anything to have a family, even just one parent, anyone who cared about me. I'm sure Johnny loves you very much. He needs you.'

'I'm the only parent he has, most of the time. He's used to his mother vanishing for weeks on end.'

'But she does come back, surely?' Pippa took a deep breath, 'And it won't help if you start having affairs too.'

Randal Harding gave her a wry smile. 'You're older than you look, aren't you? Wiser, too. Of course you're right. I don't want to do anything that might hurt my boy.' He smoothed back a tousled strand of hair from her face, his fingers caressing. 'Or you, Pippa, I don't want to hurt you, either. But I think I'm falling in love with you.'

He knew she was in love with him, and felt a quiver of warning.

'You're so sweet and gentle,' he whispered. 'I can't help wanting you.' He leant his head to kiss her again, but she drew back sharply, shaking her head.

'No! You mustn't,' she hoarsely said, and he looked at her with a new possessiveness.

'You want me, too, don't you, Pippa?'

There was a passionate curve to his mouth that made her afraid—afraid she wouldn't be able to go on rejecting him for long. She wanted him too much. The beat of desire in her blood warned her that sooner or later, if he kept kissing her, she would give in to him. She couldn't bear the idea of becoming his secret mistress; it would make her so ashamed.

She gave her notice to Miss Dalton the following Friday. It was accepted with a triumphant smile. Miss Dalton thought she had won. Her hostile tactics had scored a victory. Pippa allowed her to think whatever she chose. She didn't care. All that mattered now was to get away from Randal before it was too late.

He had left the day before, to spend a week at a business conference in the States. By the time he returned Pippa had left the firm. She had left the area, too—given up her room, moved into central London, got a job in the insurance company for which she now worked, and had found another one-room flat in

Islington, where she'd stayed until she had saved enough to buy her own home in Whitstall with the company's help. She hadn't kept in touch with anyone at Randal's firm; she didn't want him to know where she had gone, so she had had no news of him.

Until now...

Four years had made few changes in him, although his face seemed harder, more sardonic. That brooding look she remembered seemed darker, more stormy. Was his wife still having affairs? Maybe Randal had had some too, now. He couldn't have been without a woman for four years.

She felt much older, much more in control of herself as she told him, 'You're married and I'm getting married next week!'

'I'm not married any more,' he said, and her stomach seemed to drop out of her in shock.

CHAPTER THREE

EYES open wide, she stared at him in disbelief. 'You're not married any more? What do you mean?'

He smiled dryly. 'Renata left me two years ago, ran off with a golf champion she met in Scotland. She's always had an obsession with golf. Having landed a champion at the peak of his earning capacity, she wanted to hang on to him for good. She didn't just want to have an affair; she was determined to marry him. She asked me for a divorce, I gave her one, and she married him the minute it was final.'

She absorbed that, watching him intently. How had he really felt when his wife asked for a divorce? He hadn't wanted to divorce her, she remembered. That had never been in his mind. Had it been a shock to him when Renata asked him to let her go?

'I didn't hear about it,' she said. 'I suppose it was mentioned in the newspapers, but I rarely read gossip columns. What about your son?'

'She left him with me.'

That shocked Pippa. What sort of mother could abandon her child without a backward glance? Of course, Mrs Harding had spent very little time with her son, according to Randal—had she preferred to leave the boy behind, or had Randal made that a condition of agreeing to the divorce?

He added a little contemptuously, 'Renata told me her new husband didn't want a child around, cramping his style. They lead a very busy social life off the gold course; children aren't part of their scene. But then Renata was never a devoted mother, anyway.'

That, too, she remembered. 'So he lives with you now,' she thought aloud.

Randal grimaced. 'That would be difficult to manage unless I hired someone to take care of him. I have to go away so much. No, he's at boarding school in Buckinghamshire, and he likes it, thank heavens.'

'Poor little boy, he must have been upset.' The trauma of divorce always hurt the children most, didn't it?

Randal shook his head. 'I don't think he was that bothered, as far as his mother was concerned. It didn't mean he saw her less—how could he? She was rarely at home anyway. He had the stability of knowing I'd always be there for him. If he had preferred to be at home I'd have got him a full-time nanny, but he wanted to go to boarding school. One of his friends had been at his place for a year and Johnny thought it sounded great. He has lots of friends around day and night, all the things kids love—computers, sport, a swimming pool—and he's doing well in class. Oddly enough, his new stepfather has a sort of cachet, too. Sports heroes in the family are assets. The other boys envy him. Renata and her new husband visited the school and Johnny was thrilled. I'm going to visit him, myself, this weekend. I'm allowed to take him out of school at weekends; I try to do that at least once a month.'

'Well, give him my love.' She went pink. 'Not that he'll remember me, of course.' She had often thought about Johnny; strange to think that he had never even met her.

'No, you never saw him, did you? It's time you did. You must come with me at the weekend.'

She stiffened, eyes hurriedly moving away from him. 'Well, I would have loved to, he sounds a lovely little boy, but this Saturday is my wedding day, you know.'

'Ah, yes,' he drawled. 'Your wedding day. I'd forgotten that. And you're going to marry that insurance man? You can't be serious!'

She resented the ironic note in his voice, the mocking smile curling his lip. Flushed and angry, she bit back, 'Perfectly serious! You don't know Tom. Don't talk about him that way.'

'I met him, remember? I have a very shrewd idea what he's like.'

She didn't like the way he said that; he was coldly dismissive of Tom. 'He wasn't himself. The accident upset him.' She turned towards the door. 'Look, I really must be going.'

She started to walk away, but at that second somebody knocked at the outer door of the suite, calling, 'Room Service!'

'Come in,' Randal replied, and she heard a key turn then the door opened and a waiter pushed a loaded trolley into the sitting room, gave both of them a polite smile.

'Where shall I set the table up, sir?'

'Over by the window,' Randal told him, and the man wheeled the trolley over there, lifted the flaps which formed a table, began moving food around on the table surface, placed two chairs.

'Leave it. We'll help ourselves, thanks,' Randal said.

'Would you sign this for me, sir?' the waiter asked, presenting him with a pen and the bill.

Randal signed, tipped him, and the man departed. Pippa began drifting after him but didn't get very far. Randal's long fingers took her arm, held her firmly.

'No, you don't. You're staying. We have a lot to talk about yet.'

'We don't have anything to talk about!'

'I'm not married any more,' he reminded her, still holding her arm with all the potential force of those long, sinewy fingers, reminding her that if she tried to break free he was capable of resisting any effort she made.

'That has nothing to do with me!' she denied, trying not to sound too disturbed by that contact. 'Please let go of me!'

Instead, he swung her round, closer to him, his long leg touching hers. 'You were enchanting when you were twenty,' he managed, his grey eyes sliding over her in slow, sensual appraisal. 'You're gorgeous now. I just can't imagine you with the insurance salesman—how does he handle all that fire? With tongs, at arm's length?'

She didn't like the intimacy of the questions, and especially she didn't want him analysing her relationship with Tom.

To silence him she pulled free and sat down at the table. 'This looks good, all of it. What are you going to have? Some of this beef, or some cheese?'

He laughed softly. 'Trying to distract me, Pippa?' Bending, he brushed his lips along the curve of her throat, sending a shiver through her whole body. 'You're easy to read, you know.'

Was she? The remark was alarming. She must defend herself better, refuse to let him pick up her reactions. It was dangerous to let him know... She shut her eyes in dismay, refusing to continue with that line of thought, refusing to admit what it was she did not want him to know.

He stayed there for a moment, their profiles almost touching, watching her sideways, trying to gauge her expression, then at last he straightened, walked to the chair at the other side of the table and sat down opposite her.

'You help yourself, while I inspect what we have here.'

Eyes lowered, still trembling after the touch of his mouth on her skin, the scent of his body, she took more salad, a little cheese, a slice of chicken breast, a little mayonnaise, then a piece of the wholewheat bread. When she offered Randal the glass salad bowl, without looking at him, he took it, saying, 'I haven't eaten all day. All I had for breakfast was coffee and orange juice.'

'They say you should always have breakfast. Have you been staying here long?'

'No, I've been at another long conference. I seem to spend a lot of time at them.' He helped himself to wholegrain mustard. 'I don't spend much time in my own home.'

'Do you still live in the same house?' Making polite small talk helped to pass the time and she hoped it would lighten the atmosphere, making her nerves less tense, the situation seem less threatening. After all, what threat did he pose to her. He might make a pass, but she only had to reject him; he wasn't the type to turn dangerous.

Was he?

What did she know about him, though? She had known him for a few weeks, five years ago. How did she really know what sort of man he was?

'No, I moved to a flat; it made life simpler. Someone comes in twice a week to clean. I eat out a lot, or have a salad, or scrambled eggs—something I can cook myself. Johnny has a room of his own in the flat, of course, but he's only there during the school holidays. He seems to like it, though.'

'Have you actually asked him if he minded moving home, as well as going away to school?'

He shot her a wry glance. 'No, I haven't—you think I should?'

Pippa shrugged. 'It's a bit late now; you've presented him with a *fait accompli*. But next time you take a major decision that will affect him, I'd certainly ask him first.'

He leaned back in his chair, surveying her with half-lowered lids. 'If I wanted to get married again, for instance?'

Her eyes opened wide. 'Well…yes…' Her heart skipped a beat; her skin turned cold. 'Is that on the cards? Are you thinking of marrying again?' Not Miss Dalton? She thought, aware of a sense of shock. No, it must be someone new.

'Maybe,' he drawled. 'Do you think I should consult my son before committing myself?'

'Does he know her?'

'Not yet.'

'Well, I should make sure they get on well before you make any definite decision.'

She concentrated on her food, angrily conscious of a burning pain inside her stomach whenever she thought of Randal marrying again. It was stupid to be jealous—she had no right to care what he did. She was getting married herself. It was four years since she had worked in his office, four years since she had seen him, talked to him, been crazy enough to let him kiss her. A lot had happened to her in the years since then. She had grown up, learnt a lot more about the world. She had been a romantic, wide-eyed, innocent child four years ago. Now she was a woman and Randal Harding was nothing to her.

'How long have you known your insurance salesman?' he asked, and she looked up, her heart crashing like an exploding plane as she met those brilliant grey eyes.

How could she keep telling herself he was nothing to her if her body kept betraying her every time she met his eyes? The minute she'd seen him again, the night of the accident, she had been instantly overwhelmed by those old feelings. She had tried to convince herself she had forgotten him, but she had been lying.

'Four years,' she said curtly.

'Since you ran away from me, in other words?'

'I didn't run away!' she crossly denied, resenting the way he put it.

'You walked?' he dryly mocked.

'I just decided to get another job,' she corrected, her green eyes defying him. How dared he talk to her like that when he was planning to get married again himself? 'And I found this job with the insurance company, and started working for Tom.'

'How long before you went out with him?'

She bristled, her face hot, her nerves jumping. 'Why do you keep on at me like the Inquisition? My private life is nothing to do with you at all.' It had, in fact, been a very long time before she accepted a date with Tom, but she knew what Randal would make of that confession, so she was not going to admit it.

'Are you in love with him?'

'I'm not answering any more questions!' She leaned over and picked up the coffee pot. 'I'm going to have some coffee—would you like some?'

'Please. Black, no sugar.'

She poured the coffee and gave him his cup, took her own cup over to the couch. As she sat down and put her cup on the coffee table in front of her she realised she should have sat down in a chair, but it was too late. Randal had followed her and was sitting down beside her, his long legs stretched out, one thigh touching hers. She would have felt stupid if she had got up and moved to a chair; it would have been some sort of betrayal.

'If you aren't in love with him, why are you marrying him?' he murmured.

'I didn't say I wasn't in love with him!'

'Ah, but you didn't say you were! And that was as good as an admission.'

'I didn't answer because you had no right to ask the question!'

'If you were in love, why wouldn't you want to admit it?'

Conversation with him was like trying to make your way through a minefield. She was terrified of every step. Furiously, she looked round at him, glaring. 'Will you stop asking me questions?' But that was a mistake, too, because he was closer than she had realised. She found herself looking into grey eyes which were just inches away, and swallowed convulsively.

'What's the matter, Pippa?' he silkily asked.

'Nothing! I don't know what you mean!' she blustered.

'Oh, yes, you do,' he whispered, and before she could back away his head swooped down; his mouth took hers with fierce demand.

She struggled in a desperate effort to get away, but his body shifted to hold her back against the couch, his wide shoulders pinning her down. She pushed him away without making any impact on him at all. He was far too powerful and she was shaking too much to be able to make him shift.

The heat of his mouth was burning her up. Her lips parted, her eyes closed, her pulses beating wildly.

It was like rushing back through time to the day when he last kissed her; she couldn't think, could only feel, given up entirely to the pleasure and intense sweetness of his mouth on hers, his body lying across her. Her hands went round his neck and closed in his thick, dark hair. The pressure of his chest, his thighs, deepened; his fingers caressed and stroked, moving from her shoulders to her breasts, awakening her body to sensations she had never felt before. She wanted to be naked in his arms, to feel his touch with even more intensity.

From time to time in the last four years she had had dreams like this, woken from deep sleep drowsily, still trembling from the passion of his kiss, lain there crying, aching. She had suppressed the memory of those dreams, refused to think about them, or him, and gradually they had come less often—but they had not stopped entirely, and now they were visiting her again, but this time the dream was reality. This time she was in his arms, giving in to the temptation to kiss him back, to yield.

Randal lifted his mouth slowly to look down at her. Pippa kept her own eyes shut, trembling violently. She dared not meet his stare. She knew what he would be seeing, how she must look to him—weak, flushed, her mouth still parted and swollen from his kisses, still drowning in the desire pulsing through her.

'Now tell me you love him,' he huskily challenged.

She forced her eyes open, their pupils distended with passion. 'I'm going to marry him!'

'You must be insane. You won't be happy, either of you. He'll soon realise you don't love him and then he's going to hate you. He'll feel conned, trapped, and your lives together will be hell.'

'You don't know enough about us to make a prophesy like that!'

'I know about bad marriages,' he said flatly, and she winced.

'Just because you had a bad marriage doesn't mean Tom and I will. We're very different people. Tom's sweet and kind and caring, and I wouldn't hurt him for worlds. I certainly won't have affairs with other men. I'm not the type.'

'I could have an affair with you,' he said huskily, his mouth brushing the soft lobe of her ear, and she shuddered.

'Don't kid yourself! You may be vain enough to think you only have to snap your fingers to get any woman you want, but you wouldn't get me!'

'I just did,' he whispered. 'A minute ago you were in my arms and you weren't struggling. I could have got your clothes off and had you, don't deny it. It was me who called a halt, not you.'

'That's not true!' But she knew it was, and that made her even angrier, with herself as well as him. She had briefly tried to push him away, but once his mouth touched hers she had collapsed, shaking and in near delirium, kissing him back with all the passion of her dreams.

She had never felt like that about Tom. She liked Tom, admired and respected Tom, but she didn't burn with desire for him and if she was strictly honest she knew she never would. But she wasn't telling Randal that; it was no business of his how she felt about the man she meant to marry. Who did he think he was?

He smiled at her, and her head swam. 'You know it's true, Pippa. After I stopped kissing you, you just lay there with your eyes shut—what were you doing? Waiting for me to kiss you again?'

'I was too horrified to move!'

His eyes narrowed, hardened. 'What?'

'You'd scared me stiff! I was terrified of what you might do next.'

His mouth was tense with rage. 'You little liar! You weren't scared; you loved having me kiss you!'

'I hated it!' she flung back recklessly, too angry with him now to care what she said, beginning to get up, intending to make a dash for it, escape from the hotel suite.

Randal's arms closed round her and dragged her back down on the couch. 'We'll see about that,' he softly murmured, and began to kiss her again, his mouth sensually coaxing, sending waves of heat and dangerous pleasure through her.

Afraid of losing control, she gasped out, 'You're

hurting me!' and grabbed a fistful of his black hair, yanking it violently. 'Stop it!'

His lips lifted and he grimaced down at her. 'No, you're hurting me! Let go of my hair before you pull half of it out!'

'Serves you right!' she muttered, her fingers releasing the thick strands she was gripping.

They stared at each other, faces very close, breathing thickly.

'I want to leave,' she said shakily, looking away because being so close to him made her physically weak. 'Stop this, Randal. Let me go.'

He leaned down and gently, lightly, brushed his mouth over hers. 'Very well. I'll drive you home.'

'There's no need to! I can take a train.' The very prospect of having him drive her made her nerves jump violently. She had to get away from him; she couldn't take much more.

'I'm driving you,' he insisted. 'I'm curious. I want to see where you've been living. I hope it's better than that place you had when you worked for me. That wasn't fit for human habitation. Do you still live in one room?'

'No, I have a cottage,' she said with pride. She loved her home. What would he think of it? She had to admit she would rather like him to see it.

His brows rose. 'Do you rent it?'

Her chin lifted. 'No, I'm buying it on a mortgage.'

'Really? Your salary must be good.'

'I'm earning far more money now, and the insurance company helped me buy my cottage. It's company policy to assist staff to buy their own property; they feel it makes us more contented, so they give us low-interest loans.'

'And it ties you to the company?' he cynically suggested. 'So, what happens if you change jobs, move to another firm?'

'The interest goes up to the average rate and you can't blame them for that. After all, why should they continue to help you if you've left them? But you can continue with the mortgage, just like anyone else.'

'Where will you live, after the wedding?'

'At the cottage. Tom lives on an estate; his place isn't as nice as mine.'

He stood up. 'Well, let's go. Sure you don't want any of that fruit? You could take some with you.'

She shook her head. 'No, thanks. I ate more than enough.'

They left the suite and took the lift down to an underground car park. She saw Randal's car immediately: sleek and red with a long bonnet and streamlined curves. The last time she'd seen it there had been scratches and bumps all over the front, but there were none there now.

'It looks as good as new. I hope it didn't cost too much to have it repaired.'

'It had some bumps hammered out, but it didn't cost the earth.' He opened the passenger door and helped her into it, walked round and slid in beside her, behind the wheel.

The journey took nearly an hour. Traffic was heavy at this time of day through the city; they kept getting trapped in crowded streets with lines of other vehicles. Randal didn't say much. She tried not to look at him, but was deeply conscious of him beside her, those long slim legs stretched out, his elegant hands moving on the wheel. Pippa had to shrink down into

her own seat to avoid any contact with him; the car
was small and he was very close.

Eventually, though, they emerged in flat Essex
countryside and through the open window beside her
she felt cool, fresh air on her hot face, blowing her
chestnut hair about. She stared out at the hedges of
hawthorn, just coming into leaf, which in a month or
so would be thick with white flowers, at the green
fields and trees, the villages through which they
passed, some with ancient timbered cottages or white-
frame wooden churches in tidy churchyards where old
yew trees stood, bearing testimony to the long-
forgotten tradition of planting yew in churchyards so
that bows could be made from it, at old pubs with
swinging signs.

Everything looked so normal and familiar. Only
she was altered; she did not know herself. Deep inside
her panic surged. Her life was in confusion, like a
landscape after an earthquake, the earth blown apart,
wrecked, destroyed.

'Which road do I take now?' Randal asked and,
pulling herself together, she gave him directions.

'It isn't far; we should be there in ten minutes.'

'Do you like living in the country?'

'I love it.'

He was driving slowly as they passed the junction
where the accident had happened the other night. His
sideways glance told her he remembered the place.

'Where had you been?' she asked. 'That night?'

'I had been having dinner with a business associate.
I got lost; I don't know this part of the country.'

They drove on and a few moments later were park-
ing outside her cottage. He turned his head to
stare at it.

'Well, thank you for driving me home,' she huskily said, opening the passenger door.

He got out and came round to help her, his hand firmly gripping her arm. 'It's a pretty place. Have you redecorated since you bought it?'

'Yes,' she said. Afraid her neighbours might see him, be curious about him.

'I'd love a guided tour.'

In agitation she shook her head. 'I'd rather not ask you in! I expect Tom will call in on his way home from work; he'll be anxious about why I came home early. I usually come home with him. He lives quite nearby.'

Randal locked his car with a remote control, still holding her arm, then guided her towards the cottage. 'It's only half past four. He won't arrive yet, will he? He looked the type to keep long hours at work. You've got time to show me round.'

'Why are you so maddening?' she fumed. 'Why do you always have to turn everything into a battle, and win?'

He laughed softly. 'Why do you? What is your problem? Whatever I ask you to do, you argue!'

She unlocked her front door, choked with irritation. 'I just want you to go away! You know that!' Samson appeared from the flowerbeds and brushed past both of them, heading for the kitchen and, he hoped, food.

Randal smiled an amused taunt. 'Oh, I know that, but I'm not going, Pippa. I intend to save you from yourself.'

She swallowed, face disturbed. She didn't like the sound of that. What was he plotting? There was a brightness, a mischief in his eyes, that made her feel threatened. Did he intend to stay here, confront Tom, perhaps tell Tom…? Tell him what, though? They had never been lovers. There was nothing to tell. A kiss or two, that was all. She had fled before any affair could start.

And of course that was an admission in itself, because if she had not been afraid of what might develop between them she would never have been driven to flight. Would Tom realise that?

He would if Randal drew him pictures, she grimly admitted, and no doubt that was precisely what Randal intended to do. Would Tom be shocked when he discovered she had been in love before they met?

She had never lied to him, yet she had never told him anything about Randal; she had never even mentioned his name.

He looked around at the black wood beams. 'How old is the cottage?'

'The deeds date form the eighteenth century, but there was a dwelling here before that, judging by old maps of the area.' She looked at the green glass clock on the mantelpiece which she had bought in a local antiques shop. 'Tom will be here before long. Would you mind going? I want to have a shower and change before Tom gets here.'

He took no notice, wandered around the room, looking at ornaments, books, taking them out of the white-painted shelves and flipping through them, went to the window, stared out at the back garden, then walked through into the kitchen. Crossly she followed and found him opening cupboards, inspecting the inside of the fridge. Samson excitedly cavorted around him.

'Nice cat,' Randal said, scratching behind Samson's ear. 'I like the way your kitchen is laid out;

the colour scheme is very cheerful. It must be a pleasure to come in here on winter mornings.'

'You aren't planning to make me an offer for the place, are you?' she tartly enquired, and he gave her a teasing grin.

'I'm just curious about how you live. I'm trying to imagine you here. Are you always alone, or does the fiancé spend some nights here with you?'

Hot blood ran up her face. 'I told you, I'm not discussing Tom or our relationship with you!'

His grey eyes probed her face. 'You don't sleep with him, do you?' He sounded cool enough, yet something in the way he stood, body tense and alert, made her nervous. She wished she knew what he was thinking, what he was planning.

'None of your business!'

He took a step towards her and suddenly she was terrified. Turning on her heel, she ran out, up the stairs, into her bedroom and bolted the door. Sinking down on her bed, she listened; would he come up here or leave?

There wasn't a sound. No footsteps on the stairs, no movement in the passage outside the door.

He must still be downstairs. Or he could have gone, let himself out of the front door soundlessly.

She swivelled to pick up a hairbrush from her dressing table and brushed her gleaming chestnut hair; it was in disarray after the drive, with the wind blowing through the open window. Getting up, she looked in her wardrobe for something to change into when she had had her shower and chose a pale green tunic dress which ended at the knees. Simple but stylish, it was one of Tom's favourites among her clothes.

She opened drawers, found clean lingerie, laid it all

on her bedside cabinet, then went to the door and
listened with her ear against the panel.

Still silence. She carefully opened the door and
froze in shock, finding Randal leaning there; in a second he was halfway into the room and she fell back,
breathless.

'Go away!'

His gaze ran round the room, absorbing the delicate
pastel colours of the walls, the pretty curtains which
matched exactly the cover over her bed, the pink car-
pet and the white and gilt furniture.

'Charming. Did you say you decorated it all yourself?'

'Go away,' she repeated, her heart in her mouth. 'I
don't want you here.' He was taller than she remembered, his head towering over her in this little room,
the masculine force of his physical presence disturbing.

'Why did you come upstairs, if you didn't want me
to follow you? You knew I would.'

She gave him an icy, resentful look. 'I was hoping
you would take the hint and leave my house.'

'You aren't a very convincing liar, Pippa,' he
mocked, coming nearer, his grey eyes wandering possessively over her. 'Were you going to take your
clothes off? Don't let me stop you.' Leaning over, he
picked up a filmy white slip from the cabinet. 'I can't
wait to see you wearing this.'

'No,' she whispered, shuddering at the way he was
looking at her.

'Yes,' he silkily said, dropping the slip and reaching for her at the same moment.

She couldn't breathe, her throat painful, making a
sound somewhere between a sob and a groan. She

wanted him and at the same time was afraid of him.
Inside her desire and fear fought, but desire was win-
ning and she knew it.

'Don't,' she begged, her legs giving way under her,
and he picked her up bodily and carried her to the
bed.

Her eyes closed, she arched helplessly towards him
as he kissed her with sensuous insistence, his hands
exploring, caressing. She lost all consciousness of
what he was doing, her own instincts driving her. She
needed to touch him, open his shirt and discover the
power of his naked flesh and muscle, clasp his nape
and stroke his hair. She had dreamt of doing this, over
and over again, and now she was doing it.

Above her she felt the ragged beating of his heart,
his skin on hers.

Confusion flooded her mind—how could she feel
his skin on hers? Opening her eyes, she looked down
and realised he had undressed her somehow; she was
naked, her slip, her bra and panties all gone. While
she had been preoccupied with touching him he had
been stripping her.

'Pippa,' he moaned, burying his head between her
breasts, kissing the deep cleft.

He was naked, too, she realised in shock. He must
have taken off his own clothes as well as hers—how
had he done that without her knowing what was happening?

Or hadn't she wanted to know?

His mouth closed over her breast, drawing a nipple
inside the warm wetness, sucking softly.

Pleasure overwhelmed her; her arms went round
him, holding him closer; she stroked his long, naked

back and felt his knees nudging her thighs apart, his body sliding between them.

'I want you badly,' Randal groaned, and at that instant she heard a muffled sound from the door.

Stiffening, she raised herself to look past Randal. He turned his head, too.

Tom stood in the open doorway, face rigid, grey, staring.

CHAPTER FOUR

THE silence seemed endless. Pippa wished she would fall through the floor; she couldn't meet Tom's eyes. She was icy cold, shivering and sick in spite of the warmth of Randal's body lying on top of her, hiding much of her nakedness.

What could she say to him?

Even worse, what was Tom going to say to her?

In fact, he said nothing, simply turned on his heel and walked out without a word, although his body language was very vocal: the stiffness of his back, the way his head was carried, the way his arms were held, his hands clenched at his sides.

Randal whistled softly. 'Oh, dear. I suppose he has a key? And let himself in? If he'd had the good manners to ring the bell first we'd have had time to get our clothes on again before he walked in here. He didn't even call out, just came upstairs without warning, so he only has himself to blame for what he saw.'

Rage and resentment filled her. 'Don't you dare try to shift the blame to him! I've no doubt Tom was trying to be thoughtful. He'd been told I was ill—he didn't want to force me to get out of bed and come downstairs to let him in!'

She roughly pushed him off and scrambled out of bed, pulled on her clothes with hands that trembled while Randal watched her lazily, lying on his side, the afternoon sun gleaming on his smooth, naked shoulders, his lids half lowered

She tried to ignore him but even now her stupid body went on reacting to his, her mouth dry, her pulses hammering. Why was it that she never felt like this about Tom? Tom was physically attractive, he was a wonderful companion, she liked him——but she couldn't pretend he made her as aware as Randal could just by being there in the same room.

'At least you won't have to work out how to tell him!' he drawled.

It didn't help that he was right. She snapped back, 'There's nothing to tell!'

'Oh, come on, Pippa! It's time to stop lying—to him or yourself. He'll expect some sort of explanation! After all, as far as he knows you and I have never met. You hadn't told him about me, had you? He didn't react to my name when I gave it to him that night so I knew you hadn't told him about me. Yet when he walked in here five minutes ago he caught us making love! How are you going to talk your way out of that?'

She had no idea. 'I hate you!' she whispered before hurrying out of the room and running downstairs.

She found Tom on the point of going, his back to her, the front door wide open.

'Don't just go, Tom,' she said shakily. 'We must talk. I'm very sorry. I know how angry you must be, but…'

He turned to stare at her as if he had never seen her before. 'Angry?' he repeated in a low voice. 'Shattered, Pippa. I'm absolutely shattered. You, of all people, behaving like…like that.' His mouth writhed in distaste. 'I'd have taken an oath on it that you weren't capable of being promiscuous. If I hadn't seen it with my own eyes I'd never have believed it.'

She bit down on her lower lip, said in a smothered sob, 'I know, I'm sorry.'

Tom looked down at the floor, face tense, then walked past her into the sitting room. Pippa closed the front door and followed him. As she appeared he turned on her and grated, 'Who is he?'

She was startled—hadn't he recognised Randal? She had been certain he must have done, but of course Tom had only seen him briefly, in the dark, and he had been in shock, himself, after the accident.

'Randal Harding,' she prompted, but Tom's face remained blank.

Then he said slowly, 'I've heard that name before somewhere. Does he work at the office?'

She shook her head. 'No. The car crash the other night, remember?'

Tom stared, eyes widening. 'The car crash? My God, yes, you're right—that was the name of the fellow whose car hit ours.' He brushed his pale hair back, forehead creased, visibly thinking back. 'But...I don't understand... You didn't even speak to him that night; you stayed in the car. Don't tell me he came here today and talked his way in?' His voice deepened. 'Did he attack you? Is that what was happening just now? Was he trying to...? Pippa, what did he do to you?'

She shook her head, close to hysterical tears as it dawned on her that he was handing her the perfect alibi, making up a story for her to use. But she couldn't lie to him or put all the blame on Randal, even though he might deserve it.

She had asked him to go away and leave her alone but he wouldn't go. Briefly she was tempted to tell Tom what he clearly wanted to hear—that she was innocent, that Randal had been forcing her. But, no, she had to tell Tom the truth, however painful and embarrassing. She had lied to him by omission for the past four years, hiding a very important piece of her life from him. She had to tell the whole truth now.

'No, Tom. I know him. I knew him before the accident. I worked for him before I came to work with you.' She swallowed, very pale, holding herself rigid. 'I…we…' What should she tell him? How should she explain? She and Randal had not been lovers, but they might have been, if she hadn't left.

Tom leapt to the obvious conclusion, face grim. She had always thought of him as boyish. That young, cheerful look had gone now. 'He was your lover?'

'No!' She hesitated, making herself expound on the flat denial, because he had to understand how it had been. 'Well…no, but…he might have been. That was why I left. He was married with a child. I couldn't break that up, but I wasn't prepared to be his mistress, so I resigned and left the firm. I haven't seen him since.'

Tom ran a hand over his face, as if to expunge all trace of emotion from it before he spoke. When he did, he sounded almost calm, his voice flat, toneless. 'Why didn't you tell me the other night? You must have recognised him.'

'Yes, of course, at once.'

It had been a blinding trauma, the instant when Randal had got out of his car and she'd seen those long legs, the windblown black hair, the strong, sardonic face. Time had rushed backwards at an alarming pace. She had felt like a girl again, trembling and breathless.

'Then why didn't you tell me you knew him?'

'I couldn't bear to. I didn't know what to say. And I thought it wasn't necessary. After all, nothing had really happened. We were attracted to each other, and might have become lovers, but I went away, so it didn't happen. There was nothing to tell. And I didn't think I'd ever see him again after that night.'

'But today you did.'

'Yes.'

She knew what he must be thinking—and she couldn't blame him. She hadn't set eyes on Randal for four years until the accident, and today they had ended up naked in bed together within hours. Tom was justified in being shocked. She was shocked herself. She had thought she knew herself pretty well, could predict how she would behave in any given situation. She had had to learn that there were depths of her nature she hadn't had any idea about. But, after all, how well did anyone know themselves?

'I really am sorry, Tom. I never guessed what would happen,' she stammered, very flushed.

'Are you saying he did force you?'

She wished she could say yes, but shook her head. 'No, he didn't use force—he's devious and scheming, but never violent.'

Randal had had no need to use force. He had used her own feelings and desires against her and had a walk-over because she was too weak to defend herself. Whatever she might say to him, however fiercely she rejected him, Randal had some way of seeing past all that and realising his power over her.

Tom took a long, rough breath. 'What exactly are you telling me, Pippa? That you're in love with him?'

She bit her lip, staring back in helpless silence.

Tom slowly nodded. 'And not with me. You've

always said so and that's the truth, isn't it? You'll never be in love with me.'

Pippa still couldn't find the words to answer him. She could not lie, and yet how could she tell the honest to God truth without hurting him even more?

'Well, say something!' Tom shouted, his face white. 'Surely you can say something! Aren't I entitled to that, at least?'

Moistening her lip with the tip of her tongue, she took a deep breath, whispered, 'Tom...I'm so sorry...I don't know what to say. But it isn't love, that isn't what I feel for him, I don't even know what it is I do feel. Only that I don't seem able to control it.'

He laughed mirthlessly. 'And all this time I've been putting you on a pedestal. I was waiting until we were married before I laid a finger on you, because I thought you were a virgin, pure as driven snow. And now, less than a week before our wedding, I find you in bed with a stranger!'

'I'm s...' she began, and Tom suddenly shouted at her.

'Don't keep saying that!'

For a second she felt danger in him, a rage surging under his pale skin, making his body tense. She even thought he was going to hit her, and as their eyes met she knew she was thinking that too, but in the end Tom's basic decency won out and his shoulders sagged. He turned away from her to stare out of the window.

After a minute's silence that felt more like hours, he said, 'So what now? The wedding's off, I presume? Do you want me to deal with all the cancellations and phone calls? It would be better coming from me.'

'What...what will you say?'

'I'll tell the truth. We've changed our minds at the eleventh hour.' There was another pause, then he said abruptly, 'Will you be okay?'

She was touched by his concern. 'Yes,' she whispered.

'Goodbye, then.'

Spinning on his heel, he walked out of the room. She stood there, listening to him going, feeling limp and exhausted. The front door quietly closed.

It was so sudden, this ending—a week ago they had been busy planning the last details of their wedding, yet now there would be no wedding.

Her brows knit. What about her job? Tom had said goodbye—had he meant she no longer had a job? His words had sounded so final and she wouldn't be surprised if he had been firing her by implication.

How could they work together after this? The office gossip was going to be horrendous. Humiliating for Tom. The girls were going to be sorry for him, and, worst of all, show it, which he would hate. And if she went back, it would be embarrassing for her, too. People would whisper behind their backs, stare whenever they met them; some would drop hints, even have the cheek to ask direct questions.

Why? Why call the wedding off? Is there someone else? Have you met another guy? Or has Tom found another woman?

She shuddered, imagining it. No, she couldn't bear to go back and face Tom's hurt eyes, his wounded bride, or one of those curious, insolent interrogations.

Tomorrow she would have to write, resigning, and

then she would put her cottage on the market and move again. A sigh wrenched her. Last time there had been no problem moving home, that shabby little room hadn't mattered to her, but this time she was bitterly reluctant to leave her home, the cottage she had spent so much time and energy and money on improving. It had been the very first real home she had ever had. She did not want to leave it. But she knew she couldn't stay here, not now.

Standing at the window into the back garden, she watched sunlight sparkling on spring flowers: the few last white narcissi, pale, frail flowers, purple hyacinth, whose fragrance made them hypnotic for insects which buzzed between them, making deep splashes of colour against the green of the lawn, newly budding bluebells under the apple tree not yet in blossom. She would probably never see another spring here.

Tears filled her eyes. She leaned on the window frame, put her hands over her eyes, weeping.

The first she knew of Randal's arrival was when he took hold of her shoulders and turned her towards him, one hand behind her head, pushing her face into his chest. She was too miserable to protest or struggle; she desperately needed comfort. Weakly, she lay against him, sobbing.

His fingers stroked her hair, rubbing her scalp in a sensuous rhythm she found hypnotic. 'Was he very unpleasant?'

She drew breath, said shakily, 'Not at all. I almost wish he had been. He was hurt, which was far worse. I feel so guilty.'

Randal put a finger under her chin and lifted her head, stared down into her tear-wet green eyes. 'You didn't love him and he'd have realised it eventually after you married him, and then he'd have been a damn sight more hurt. Surely you see that?'

She didn't answer, her mouth trembling. Randal put his thumb on it and traced the weak curve, caressed her upper lip, watching her like a cat watching a mouse. To her, his grey eyes seemed cruel, predatory.

'I think you'd better go now,' she said, eyes flaring with hostility.

His arms tightened round her and he bent his head to take her mouth fiercely. The heat of the kiss melted her anger, made her knees give way under her, but she didn't mean to let him do this to her again. She had to get control of herself—and him.

She grabbed his shoulders to push him away but couldn't move him. It was like trying to push over a rock.

Abandoning the attempt, she meant to let her hands fall, but his kiss deepened, invading her parted mouth. A groan broke from her. Her fingers curled instinctively and she found herself holding on as if she was clinging to the only thing that would stop her collapsing on the floor.

Randal murmured thickly, pulling her even closer, and lifted her off her feet. A second later she was lying on the couch, still held in his arms, her body on top of his, his hand grasping her head, holding it still, while he went on kissing her with a devouring passion that turned her blood to fire.

When he lifted his head she couldn't move, her green eyes drowsy and half closed, breathing thickly as she stared down at him, her body aching with pleasure.

'You see? You're mine,' he whispered. 'It would

have been a crime if you had married that poor fellow. He deserves a wife who loves him. It was kinder for him to find out, even if the shock did hurt him. He'll get over it and find somebody else, and be happier with her than he could ever have been with you.'

She closed her eyes and let her head fall on to his chest, feeling the deep reverberations of his heart under her face, the rise and fall of his breathing.

'I take it the wedding is definitely off?' he quietly asked, and she nodded.

'Yes, Tom said he would see to the cancellation of all the arrangements.' A wry, painful smile twisted her lips. 'He's a bit of a control freak; he doesn't trust me to take care of it myself.'

'Why were you crying?'

She sighed. 'For Tom...'

'You never loved him! Admit it!'

'No, but he loved me and I've hurt him. Also, I've realised I have to sell this cottage, and I love it so much. But I'll have to resign from the firm, I couldn't go on working with Tom after this, and I can't stay here once I've given up my job. I'd have to rearrange the mortgage, and I might not be able to afford a much higher mortgage.'

'You worry too much; that's your problem.'

She looked at him angrily. 'That's typical. You just brush my worries aside with a shrug. The fact is my whole life is being torn apart, for the second time, and it's all your fault again. Last time I was only living in that room, but this time I'm going to lose the first real home I've ever had.'

'Come and live with me.'

She started, drew a long, sharp breath. 'I'd rather die!'

Maddeningly, he laughed. 'I don't think you would, when it came to the moment of choice. Think about it. Die, or live with me? Now, which do you think you'd choose?'

'Oh, you think you're so funny!' She struggled, fuming. 'Will you let me up, please? I think you should be going.'

He sat up, brushing back his tousled black hair. 'Is there anywhere around here to have dinner?'

'Drive back into London,' she curtly said, getting up and tidying her clothes, her hair.

'I want to have dinner with you.'

She turned on him, eyes blazing. 'Haven't you done enough to me today? I got up this morning feeling fine, with my wedding a week away and my life arranged in front of me. Then you came along and blew it all to pieces. And now you want me to have dinner with you? The answer is no! I won't have dinner. I never want to see you again. Is that clear enough?'

He looked into her eyes and her bones turned to water inside her. 'You don't mean it. You want me as much as I want you. Why pretend you don't? We're both free now.'

She hesitated, looking down. He wasn't going to give up and go away, but she wasn't giving up, either. He had walked back into her life and broken her world apart, without caring if he hurt her, or Tom, only interested in getting his own way. He kept saying he wanted her. He hadn't said he loved her. If he loved her he wouldn't have pursued her ruthlessly when he knew she was getting married in a few days.

He hadn't even seen her for four years. He could

have had no idea whether she loved Tom or not. No idea, either, what she felt, or wanted, or thought.

That didn't matter to him. He had no respect for her, no interest in what went on inside her head, or her heart. All he cared about was her body. He was determined to have it.

That wasn't love, was it?

And she wasn't going to let him have his own way.

'Pippa,' he softly said. 'What do I have to do? Beg? Have dinner with me. We have a lot to talk about.'

They seemed to have been talking all day, getting nowhere. How could they when they weren't talking about the same thing? She had to persuade him to go away, but how? There was only one way. She must let him think he had won, must pretend to give in, then he would leave the cottage and she could escape.

'There is a country club a couple of miles away,' she murmured, and felt him smiling to himself. He thought he had won; she was going to be easy.

'Do they have a good restaurant?'

'It's quite good. English and French cooking.'

'Should I book a table? Or can we just turn up?'

'I should book.' Out of the corner of her eye she shot a look at the clock on her mantelpiece. It was half past six.

'What's it called?'

'Little Whitstall Country Club. You'll find it in the telephone book by the telephone. Or would you like me to book it?'

'No, I will.' He walked over to the phone and began flicking through the pages. She was thinking feverishly. How was she going to persuade him to leave for a while?

He made the call, put down the phone and turned to her, his gaze wandering down over her.

'I suppose you'll want to change into something more formal?'

She pretended surprise, looked down at her clothes. 'Oh…if you like…'

'There isn't time for me to go back to London to change; what I'm wearing will have to do. But I must buy some petrol. I'm not sure I'll have enough to get back to town later tonight, and all the garages will be shut by then, I suppose. Where's the nearest garage?'

'I don't know one on the way to the country club, but there is one a mile away, in the first village back from here. While you get your petrol I'll change into something more suitable.'

He smiled at her and she ached with a strange mixture of pleasure and anger. He was charming, far too charming. She didn't trust him. He meant to sleep with her tonight, after dinner. No doubt he would get her to drink a lot of wine, then he would bring her back here and talk his way into the cottage, upstairs into her bedroom, then into her bed.

Pippa wasn't even sure she had the strength of will to resist him, but if she did surrender tonight she was going to despise herself tomorrow.

'Okay, I won't be long.'

She stood there, listening to his departing footsteps, the front door closing, his car door opening and slamming again, the engine firing and then the sound of his car moving away, before she moved herself.

First she ran upstairs, found a suitcase and packed in a hurry, then she changed into jeans and sweater, carried her suitcase downstairs and put on a warm sheepskin jacket hanging in the hall. She had no idea where she was going, but she had to rush, to get away before he got back.

She knew a small hotel in Maldon, on the Thomas estuary; she had been there before. She looked up the number, rang them, booked a single room, then after hanging up she put down water and a saucer full of dried food for Samson, who had vanished again, through his catflap in the kitchen door. He could come and go as he chose, so he would be okay for a couple of days. In any case, she knew he visited several other houses nearby, where he got fed and cosseted. Cats were self-sufficient and independent.

Before leaving she carefully turned off all the lights, checked she had her credit cards and cheque-book, everything she might need. Fifteen minutes later she was in her car, driving away, being careful to take a route which would make sure she did not pass Randal's car returning.

CHAPTER FIVE

THE weather had turned chill and misty by the time she reached the little estuary town of Maldon. The weather rolled in from the sea and was funnelled up the river. She parked in the car park behind the hotel and carried her case through the bar to check in. There were a few people drinking in the bar; they mostly seemed to know each other, which meant they were either local residents who drank here or they kept a yacht at Maldon, as many people did from London and the south of the country. As Pippa passed they all turned their heads to inspect her, some murmuring comment to companions. In the summer Maldon had many visitors, but at this time of year there were far fewer.

While she was filling in the card handed to her by the small, trim receptionist, she was asked, 'Will you be having dinner tonight, madam?'

'Yes, please,' Pippa said, handing the woman the registration card.

'What time?'

Pippa glanced at her watch and was surprised by how quickly she had driven there, but then she knew the way through the winding marsh roads. She hadn't had to consult a map or slow down to check signposts.

'Eight-thirty?'

'Certainly, madam. The dining room is on the left

through the bar. Jim will take your bag upstairs for you.'

A white-bearded old man popped up from an inner office and seized Pippa's case, carried it up the wide, ancient, creaking staircase with Pippa following him, feeling guilty.

He looked old enough to be her father. She hoped the case wasn't too heavy for him.

'This was an old pub, miss, till it was modernised and turned into a hotel,' he told her. 'Hundreds of years old. There was a pub here in the Middle Ages, I'm told. A lot of local people still treat it as their pub.' He put her case down outside a door at the end of a short corridor and produced a key. 'Here you are, miss. I hope you'll be very comfortable in here.'

She looked around curiously while the porter carried her bag inside. 'TV, with remote control,' he pointed out. 'Hospitality tray, with tea and coffee, and if you want fresh milk contact Reception. The bathroom is on your right.'

She smiled. 'Thank you.' And tipped him.

He saluted and was gone, leaving her alone. She was pleased with the room; it was spacious and a little old-fashioned, all chintz and oak furniture, which she found comforting. She unpacked, put her clothes away, found the hospitality tray, which bore a kettle, tea and coffee sachets and a cup, and made herself a cup of coffee.

She drank it standing next to the window, which looked down through mist on to a quayside lined with rows of small boats. Now and again a figure moved through the mist, grey, wavering, insubstantial, like a living etching. There was the faint sound of footsteps and then the silence came back and nothing stirred except the gentle lapping of water at the quay steps.

She had half an hour before her dinner. After that long drive she felt like a walk so she put on her jacket and went downstairs, crossing the bar again to go out on to the quay. The people drinking all watched her with the same unblinking curiosity.

As she walked out of the hotel the mist swallowed her. From somewhere nearby she heard a church clock chime. That might be eight o'clock. She couldn't go far or she would be late for dinner. Wandering along the quayside, she read the names of boats. The mist was thickening; she could barely see a hand in front of her face. Shivering, she drove her hands down into her jacket pockets. There was nobody else around; she could have been marooned on a desert island, or the last person alive on earth.

A moment later, though, she heard footsteps behind her and glanced round. A tall shape loomed through the mist. She couldn't see his face but she instinctively felt him staring at her, felt a strange prickle of threat. He began to walk faster, and panic flared inside her. She quickened her steps, too, almost running, and tripped over a lobster pot someone had left on the quay.

Pippa sprawled headlong. The man behind ran to catch up and knelt down beside her. 'Did you hurt yourself?'

Shock made her speechless. She turned her head to look up at him incredulously as she recognised the voice and face. Drops of pearly mist dewed his hair and brow and he was wearing a leather jacket zipped up to the neck.

'What are you doing here?' she burst out. There

was something of black magic about his appearance out of the mist when she had thought him safely miles away.

Randal stood up, pulled her up beside him, his strong hands clasped around her waist. 'Thought you'd given me the slip, did you?' Dry mockery in his smile made her bristle.

'How did you know where I'd gone?' She was still having difficulty believing he was here. She tried to work out how he had followed her. 'Did you see me leaving when you came back from getting petrol?'

'I didn't go to get petrol,' he wryly admitted. 'I was a bit suspicious about your sudden agreement to have dinner with me. I had the feeling you were planning something so I parked just down the road, behind some trees, where I could watch your cottage without you seeing me. I had a suspicion you would try to cheat, and I was right, wasn't I? I saw you come out of your cottage and get into your car. When you drove out I followed at a discreet distance.'

It was the same trick he had played when he waited for her to come out of her office and followed her to the bridal shop. She might have guessed he wouldn't just go off to get petrol, leaving her the opportunity to escape before he returned.

It dawned on her that he was still holding on to her. She slapped his hands down and took a step back.

'Careful! You don't want to end up in the water, do you?' he said as she toppled on the edge. He took her wrists and pulled her towards him to safety.

She broke free again. 'Who do you think you are? James Bond? Why can't you leave me alone?' she broke out, trembling with rage. 'The fact that I left like that should tell you I don't want to see you. Ever again. Why don't you take the hint, and stop harassing me!'

'I'm not harassing you,' he smoothly said. 'I was worried about you, driving off in that state. You were upset over your ex-fiancé. And it was misty. You might have had a crash.'

'But I didn't!'

He shrugged his wide shoulders gracefully. 'No, you didn't. But what on earth made you chose to come to a dead and alive hole like this?'

'I like it. It's peaceful.' Shooting him a resentful look, she added pointedly, 'Normally.'

He smiled. 'Have you booked into your hotel for dinner?'

'Yes, and I must get back for it at once,' she said curtly, and began to walk fast.

Randal kept pace with her. 'I'm staying there too.'

Her heart sank, although she should have guessed. Where else?

'We can have dinner together, after all,' he triumphantly added.

She considered refusing, for a moment, but knew he would somehow make sure he won the argument and felt too tired to fight him any more. He was the most maddening man she had ever met. He wouldn't listen to her. If she ran he pursued her. He had ruined her life twice, and she had fled, but here he was again. She had a terrible suspicion that she was never going to be able to shake him off. Was she going to spend the rest of her life running away from him and being pursued?

Inside the cosy warmth of the old hotel she hurried upstairs to take off her jacket and do something about her appearance, brushed her hair, renewed her make-

up, staring at her reflection and horrified at the feverish brightness of her green eyes, the tremor in her
mouth.

He always had this effect on her. Could he see that?
How could he fail to notice the way she was shaking?

She turned away, shivering, then went downstairs
again and found the dining-room.

Randal was already seated at a table by the window
overlooking the quay, a bottle of white wine chilling
in an ice bucket beside him. He had shed his leather
jacket and was wearing a dark jacket, a crisp white
shirt and a blue silk tie. Her breath caught. Did he
have to be so good-looking, so distinguished?

He rose as she joined him. 'There you are! I was
beginning to think you had run off again.'

She sat down opposite him and glanced through the
menu, which was not extensive but sounded good; she
decided to have melon followed by grilled sole with
a salad. The waiter came to take their order, wrote
down what she wanted first, then turned to Randal,
who chose melon, steak and chips.

When the waiter had gone Randal poured wine into
her glass. 'How long do you plan to stay here?'

'I haven't decided yet.' She sipped the golden wine
and felt a little warmth come back into her veins. 'Not
long. I must go back soon and start planning. I have
to write to the insurance firm, resigning, put my cottage on the market and start looking for another job.'

'I'll give you one.'

She gave him a dry look. 'No, thank you. I don't
think that would be a good idea.'

'Why not?'

Flushed, she looked down into her wine glass, playing with the stem. 'Don't they say, ''Never go

back''?' She wished he would stop asking her these pointed questions; she didn't want to think about the reasons for the way she felt. She didn't know herself why she had these strong impulses, this desire to run from him and keep running.

'Who's they, anyway?' he asked, watching her across the table with narrowed, searching eyes.

She shrugged, looking up briefly, then down again, because she could not meet his lance-like gaze. 'Oh…people.'

'People with minds like train tracks. You should never make rules for life. Life is for living, spontaneously, on instinct. You don't need rules. You're not a machine, you're a human being, a living organism.'

She sipped more wine. 'Talking about living spontaneously, I've been thinking I might get a job aboard—Paris, say.'

There was a pause, then he asked flatly, 'Is your French good enough for that?'

'I speak a little, and if I'm living there I'd soon learn a lot more. And I've always loved the idea of living in Paris; it's such a beautiful, exciting city.'

Gravely, Randal said, 'But you'd be a foreigner, far away from home—it wouldn't be an easy life and you would have to speak French all the time. It can be difficult to be accepted into the local community. I'd think very carefully about going to work there.'

The waiter returned with their first course: a whole ogen melon, with a lid carved out like petals, golden and ripe, chilled from the fridge, filled with a medley of soft fruit—cherries, peach, strawberries steeped in liqueur. Was it Kirsch? she wondered, rolling it round her mouth.

'I wasn't expecting it to be this good,' Randal said, tasting it too.

'Neither was I,' she admitted.

'But you said you knew this place pretty well, had been here a few times.'

'That's true, but the food wasn't this good when I ate here before. Maybe they have a new chef.' She ate a cherry. 'These must be imported; you won't be able to get fresh cherries here for a couple of months. Tom and I picked cherries in Kent last June when we were staying at a farm. Of course, Kent cherries are pink and cream, not dark red, like these.'

Randal's face tightened, a frown drawing his brows together. 'You know, what I can't understand is why on earth you let yourself come so close to marrying him. Surely your common sense warned you it would be the biggest mistake of your life if you went ahead with it?'

Defiantly, she retorted, 'We could have been very happy! What do you know?'

'You weren't in love with him, and I suspect he wasn't really in love with you, either! I didn't get the impression he was sick with passion.'

She looked daggers at him. 'You don't know Tom; he's a good man.'

'Good, but boring. Oh, come on, Pippa, you know he would never set the world on fire. How could you have been happy with him? Unless all you were looking for was a nice, quiet, comfortable life with a man who wouldn't ask for too much from you.'

She finished her melon and sat back, glowering. 'Will you please stop talking about it?'

'Maybe that really is what you want? A man who won't expect too much?'

GET FREE BOOKS and a FREE GIFT WHEN YOU PLAY THE...

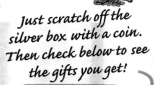

Lucky 7

Just scratch off the silver box with a coin. Then check below to see the gifts you get!

SLOT MACHINE GAME!

YES! I have scratched off the silver box. Please send me the 2 free Harlequin Presents® books and gift for which I qualify. I understand I am under no obligation to purchase any books, as explained on the back of this card.

306 HDL DFTC

106 HDL DFTA
(H-P-OS-11/01)

NAME   (PLEASE PRINT CLEARLY)

ADDRESS

APT.#   CITY

STATE/PROV.   ZIP/POSTAL CODE

7	7	7	**Worth TWO FREE BOOKS plus a BONUS Mystery Gift!**
🍒	🍒	🍒	**Worth TWO FREE BOOKS!**
♣	♣	♣	**Worth ONE FREE BOOK!**
🔔	🔔	🍒	**TRY AGAIN!**

Visit us online at www.eHarlequin.com

DETACH AND MAIL CARD TODAY!

The Harlequin Reader Service® — Here's how it works:

Accepting your 2 free books and gift places you under no obligation to buy anything. You may keep the books and gift and return the shipping statement marked "cancel." If you do not cancel, about a month later we'll send you 6 additional novels and bill you just $3.34 each in the U.S., or $3.74 each in Canada, plus 25¢ shipping & handling per book and applicable taxes if any.* That's the complete price and — compared to cover prices of $3.99 each in the U.S. and $4.50 each in Canada — it's quite a bargain! You may cancel at any time, but if you choose to continue, every month we'll send you 6 more books, which you may either purchase at the discount price or return to us and cancel your subscription.

*Terms and prices subject to change without notice. Sales tax applicable in N.Y. Canadian residents will be charged applicable provincial taxes and GST.

If offer card is missing write to: Harlequin Reader Service, 3010 Walden Ave., P.O. Box 1867, Buffalo NY 14240-1867

BUSINESS REPLY MAIL
FIRST-CLASS MAIL   PERMIT NO. 717-003   BUFFALO, NY

POSTAGE WILL BE PAID BY ADDRESSEE

HARLEQUIN READER SERVICE
3010 WALDEN AVE
PO BOX 1867
BUFFALO NY 14240-9952

NO POSTAGE
NECESSARY
IF MAILED
IN THE
UNITED STATES

Her skin was burning; she resented his comments. 'Look, thanks to you, my marriage is off so there's no point in discussing it any further, is there?'

'I'm just trying to work out your motivation,' he calmly told her, and she clenched her hands into fists on her lap, wanting to punch him.

'Mind your own business, will you? If I need a psychiatrist, I'll go and see one. I don't want you doing amateur work on my head.'

'You need to do some thinking! You're one of the most mixed-up women I've ever met! You have no idea about what goes on inside you, do you?'

She was about to snap back at him when the waiter appeared to take their plates away, so she closed her mouth and looked down while the man refilled their glasses. Pippa was startled to see she had drunk most of the white wine she had had in her glass. She had drunk it without realising what she was doing. It was strange; she had rarely before drunk much wine.

Maybe it was another way of running, fleeing from Randal Harding. She needed to muffle her senses, dull her nerve-ends. Escape.

She didn't want to think about what she needed to escape from.

As the waiter went away again Randal's supple, powerful hand stretched across the table to move the low vase of flowers between them so that he could see her more clearly.

'I'd like you to come with me to see my son—will you?'

Surprised, she looked up, green eyes wide, hesitated. 'I'm sure he would rather be alone with you. He must miss you, even if he does like the school.'

'I want him to know you, and I want you to know him.'

She stared at him, biting her inner lip. 'Oh. But...why...?'

'Johnny rarely if ever sees his mother. I think he needs women in his life; I don't want him to grow up in an all-male world. It isn't healthy.'

She couldn't argue with that. She believed children needed two parents—she knew she had needed, longed for that. 'But surely you have a sister? Or another female relative?'

She knew so little about him; his marriage had been a towering wall between them, and she had seen nothing beyond that.

Impatiently, he said, 'Why don't you want to meet my boy?'

'I didn't say I didn't it's just that I...' Her voice trailed off. How could she tell him she was afraid to meet his son in case she grew fond of him? The child had already lost his mother; it would be cruel to let him get used to her, herself, only for her to vanish too one day.

'What?' he demanded relentlessly, those grey eyes boring into her like lasers. He wasn't giving up, and she didn't have the energy for another fight, so with a sigh she gave in.

'Oh, very well.' It was easier to agree now and make some excuse when the time came than to go on arguing.

He gave her that warm, charming, triumphant smile. She regarded him dryly, understanding the triumph. He loved to win. That much she did know about him.

'Good girl,' he approved. 'I'm sure you'll like him.'

'You've never told me much about him. What's he like?'

'Me,' he said, with self-satisfaction. 'He's very like me.'

Sarcastically she murmured, 'Oh, well, I'm sure he's gorgeous, then.'

Randal looked at her through his lashes with an intimate, mocking amusement, making her heart knock at her ribcage; she expected him to make some tart come-back, but at that moment their main course arrived and they began to eat.

They spoke very little; she wondered if he was silent because he had achieved his objective in getting her to agree to meet his son, and no longer had much to say. That would be typical of him; he was a very focused man, concentrated on getting his own way.

When they had finished their main course Randal asked if she would like a pudding, but she shook her head.

'If I eat any more I'll never be able to sleep tonight.'

He nodded. 'I won't have anything else, either. Coffee?'

'No, that might keep me awake, too.' It was half past ten by then, and she couldn't stop yawning, so she was sure she would sleep, but coffee might be a mistake.

'Tired?'

She yawned again, nodded. 'Sorry. It has been a fraught day. I've used up all my energy.' She rose. 'I must get some sleep; I'll have a lot to do tomorrow. I'll go home, write to the insurance company and resign, and tell them I'm selling my home, then I must talk to an estate agent and put the cottage on the market.'

They walked up the wide, creaking stairs together a few minutes later. 'What time shall we have breakfast?' he asked, and she looked at him impatiently.

'You have it whenever you like!'

'I want to have it with you,' he said in a coaxing voice, giving her that smile.

'How do I know what time I'll wake up? I didn't ask for a wake-up call. I may sleep late.' They arrived at her door. Her key in her hand, she faced him, chin up. 'Goodnight.'

'Goodnight,' he said, turning away.

She breathed a little easier; she had had an uneasy feeling he might not go too readily and had been nerving herself for a fight. He turned the corner in the corridor and his footsteps faded. Putting the key in the lock, she opened the door and began to go into her room. A second later Randal was inside too and the door was shut. She hadn't even heard him coming.

Angrily, she blazed at him. 'Get out! How dare you? Do I have to scream the place down?'

Randal grabbed her by the shoulders and kissed her hungrily, his mouth a sensual temptation. Head swimming, eyes closed, she swayed in his arms, trying desperately not to go under, struggling not to surrender to the physical glamour of his kiss, his touch, his body pressing against hers.

The trouble was, she could never fight her attraction to him. She might stay cool and collected when he was talking to her—she could fight her feelings so long as he didn't touch her. But as soon as she was in his arms she felt herself weakening, yielding to the powerful erotic sensations he awoke in her. Her mind could not control her body. She felt as though her brain was submerged beneath some level of consciousness her waking mind could not reach. She was helpless in the grip of a desire that beat inside her, deep and harsh and driven, sending wild vibrations through her and silencing all rational thought.

Slowly, Randal pulled his head back and looked down at her, and Pippa opened her eyes to stare back at him, shuddering.

'You kiss me like that, and yet you keep pretending you don't want me?' he whispered. 'What's going on inside that head of yours? We're both free now, there's nothing to keep us apart—so why are you still fighting it?'

CHAPTER SIX

SHE had asked herself the same question, ever since they'd met again, and she still wasn't sure of the answer. They were both free now, as he said. She wanted him, she couldn't deny it—and yet...

And yet for some reason she found herself backing away every time they came too close, and she didn't know why.

'You're moving too fast,' she guessed aloud without real conviction, pushing at his shoulders and taking a step back. 'We only met again less than twelve hours ago and a lot has happened since then. My marriage is off, I'm leaving my job and selling my home—the last few hours have been an emotional avalanche. I'm still reeling. The last thing I need is you trying to force the pace.'

He let go of her slowly, frowning. 'Maybe that's it. But I'm afraid you'll run away again. It's a habit of yours. And you're deceitful, Pippa. I left you getting ready to have lunch with me earlier today and what did you do? You ran away here, to Maldon. Why did you do that? Maybe that's what you're intending to do again. Maybe tomorrow morning I'll find you've skipped the hotel and gone before I get up for breakfast.'

Soberly, she said, 'I promise I won't. I give you my word.'

He studied her face intently. 'You'll meet me downstairs for breakfast? You swear?'

'I swear. What time?'

'Eight-thirty?'

She nodded. 'Eight-thirty. I'll be there. Then I'm checking out and going home to write letters and make phone calls.'

He moved towards the door. 'Okay, see you at breakfast, then.'

She followed so that she could bolt the door as soon as he had left and Randal looked down at her mockingly.

'Goodnight.' Bending briefly, he dropped a light kiss on the tip of her nose, then he was gone, and Pippa bolted the door after him. That tiny, intimate caress left a warm feeling inside her, though, while she was undressing, taking off her make-up, washing, getting into bed.

There was something special between them; there had been from the beginning. She had never felt anything like that for anyone else. Oh, she liked Tom, but ruefully she had to admit that if she had married him it would have been a disastrous mistake. She would never have loved him, really loved him.

Switching off her bedside lamp, she lay in the darkness listening to the slow lap-lap of water on the quayside, an occasional footfall out there in the damp grey mist. Above her the ancient floors creaked as someone walked across another bedroom. Pipes hummed as water ran. But otherwise the hotel was quiet, nobody seemed to be listening to television or talking, and it didn't take her long to get to sleep.

The room was full of sunlight when she woke up; the mist had obviously cleared. Slipping out of bed, she parted the curtains to peer out. The quay bristled with masts; brightly painted little boats moored in rows, bobbing against each other as the water rose and fell.

She read their names, smiling. The *True Love*; *Scrumpy Joe*; *Heggarty Peggarty*; *Sue-Anne*. Some of them had men working on them, unpacking sails, scrubbing decks, painting, coiling ropes. Along the quay sat men drinking mugs of tea or coffee. After the grey damp silence of yesterday, the quay had come alive and was full of people.

Sunshine made you feel happier. Smiling, Pippa walked into the bathroom and took a shower before getting dressed to go down to breakfast. Although she had eaten that large dinner last night, she was now hungry again, perhaps because the sunshine had lifted her spirits and she felt more positive.

She put on jeans and a bright turquoise sweater, did her make-up, then quickly packed her case before leaving the room. As she came down the ancient stairs she saw Randal sitting in a chair below, reading a newspaper and looking up every so often to check if she was on her way.

'Why are you waiting there? Why not in the dining room?' she asked him as he stood up to greet her.

'To make sure you didn't creep away without breakfast,' he coolly admitted, flicking a glance over her from head to foot before following her into the dining room.

'I promised I wouldn't!' A little flush flowed into her face at the way he had looked at her. He didn't miss a thing, from the peaks of her breasts inside the sweater to her trim waist and long legs in the tight jeans. And that look, the glitter of desire in his grey eyes, made her pulses leap and race.

He shrugged. 'I wasn't entirely sure I could trust you.'

She couldn't honestly resent that; she knew she deserved it.

They were shown to the same table they had occupied last night, and given menus. 'Tea or coffee?' asked a young waitress. 'White or brown toast?'

'Coffee,' they both chose.

'And mixed toast?' suggested Pippa. Randal nodded, and the waitress vanished to fill their order.

Breakfast didn't take up much of their time; Pippa just had a bowl of fresh fruit followed by a boiled egg with toast. Randal had porridge and a kipper. By nine o'clock they had finished, and left the dining room together.

Pippa paid her bill and asked for her suitcase to be brought down. While she was waiting for the porter Randal quietly asked, 'You're going straight to your cottage now?'

'Yes.' She took a deep breath. 'And, please, don't come there too. I have a lot to do and I would rather be alone.'

His face impassive, he turned away. 'I'd better pay my own bill; I still have to pack. You'll probably leave before I do. Drive safely.'

He hadn't promised he wouldn't come to the cottage. She looked crossly at his back as he began paying his bill. Then the porter appeared with her case. With him on her heels, Pippa walked out to the car park and a few minutes later was driving away.

This morning the marsh looked quite different; with the mist gone the horizon was bright and the fields shimmered under the sun. She drove slowly, enjoying the landscape and the sound of birds. A heron flew low, its grey profile memorable, legs trailing, fixedly gazing down at the silvery estuary in search of prey.

It was twenty past ten when she arrived home, and as she parked she saw with a jolt of shock that Tom's car was parked a few feet away. Dismay filled her. He must be in the cottage; he still had a key. Questions buzzed inside her—why was he here? At this time of day he should be at work. What did he want? He had been surprisingly low-key yesterday in his reaction, but he had had time to think about it. Had he come back to make an angry scene?

Her teeth gritted. Whether she wanted to or not, she had to face Tom; she wasn't running away, not any more. She had done too much of that with Randal. So she lifted her chin and walked towards the front door, which opened as she approached.

Tom confronted her in his dark city suit, like a grim avenging angel.

'Where have you been?' he asked with belligerence. 'It looks as if you've been out all night. Your bed wasn't slept in and everything is spotless.' He paused, then asked tersely, 'I suppose you've been with *him*?'

She walked past into the cottage, sighing. 'No, I haven't!' It wasn't exactly a lie, because Tom was really asking if she had slept with Randal, and she hadn't had she? 'I don't want a row, Tom. No inquisition, please. Why are you here?'

'I realised I had to see you to sort things out. We didn't talk properly yesterday, did we? So I took a day off work.' He followed her into the kitchen and watched her put on a kettle and start laying out cups and saucers, put teabags into the teapot.

'I thought we'd said everything, Tom.'

'We were both in shock,' he said roughly. 'Now we've calmed down and I've had time to think. Look, if you want to stay in your job, you can. There's no need to feel you have to leave. People have broken off engagements before. I'm big enough to cope with a few jokes and snide remarks. You can take time to stay on, look for another job if you still want to move, but walking out right now you wouldn't have a salary until you started work elsewhere, and I don't want you to get into financial difficulties because of me.'

She looked at him incredulously, her green eyes swimming in tears. 'Oh, Tom, that is so sweet!'

He shuffled his feet, very flushed. 'Just common sense. A broken engagement isn't the end of the world. We'll get over it. So—do you want to stay on?'

She shook her head. 'Thank you for offering, Tom, but, no, I would rather leave. You're braver than I am. I don't think I could face those jokes. I'm sure I shall get another job even if it isn't as well paid.'

'With him?'

Her eyes dropped to the floor. 'No.'

'You used to work for him, you said.'

'Yes, I did.'

With an angry bite, Tom demanded, 'But he didn't offer you a job? What a bastard. When it's his fault you need a job.'

Pippa groaned. 'Oh, Tom. Yes, he did, actually. He said I could have a job with his firm, but I'm not taking up the offer.'

Tom thought about that. 'But you and he are... getting together?'

'No! I've no intention of... No!'

He ran a hand through his hair, his face confused.
'I don't understand. I thought that was the whole
point? That you were in love with him, that that was
why you weren't going to marry me? If you aren't
going to him, then why is it off between us?'

The kettle boiled; she made the tea, her back to
him. 'It isn't that simple, Tom. Try to understand. I
know it's hard, but try. Seeing him again made me
realise I was not in love with you, and never would
be. And I couldn't go ahead with the marriage when
I knew it wouldn't work for us. Do you see?'

'No, I don't! You say you aren't going back to him,
which I suppose means you aren't in love with him—
so how did that make you realise you weren't in love
with me, either?'

'Tom...' She fumbled for the right words, helpless
to make it clear without hurting his feelings. 'Tom, I
was in love with him four years ago. Desperately in
love. I got badly hurt, but at least I knew I was doing
the right thing in going away, in not breaking up his
marriage. When you and I started seeing each other I
thought I was over all that. I'd forgotten how I felt
about Randal. I didn't try to compare the way I felt
about you with the way I had felt about him. I honestly believed we could be happy together.'

'I still think we could be!' Tom said eagerly, coming closer. 'If you aren't in love with him, we still
have a chance, Pippa.'

She picked up the teapot and poured the tea, shaking her head. 'I'm sorry, Tom, but, no, we don't have
a chance. I know now that it was wrong of me to
think I could make you happy.'

He put a hand on her back, gently stroking her
spine, and leaned his face against her thick chestnut

hair, murmuring into it, 'How can you be so sure? Two days ago, everything was fine. Then you bump into this chap and suddenly the wedding is off and you tell me we don't have a chance. But you still haven't made it clear. If you aren't in love with him either, why can't you marry me?'

She closed her eyes, groaning. 'Because I remember how I felt about him! And when I do marry, I want to feel that way again.'

He turned her round, still holding her, and softly kissed her. 'You could learn to feel that way about me, Pippa.'

She shook her head regretfully, hating to hurt him, but knowing it was kinder in the long run. 'I'm sorry, Tom. I'm very fond of you, and I like you a lot, but I know now that I could never love you the way I loved him.'

He groaned and kissed her again, harder, with pleading. 'Pippa… I don't want to lose you. I think we could be very happy together. We have been, haven't we? I always believed we were a perfect match. Are you sure you aren't chasing some impossible star? Looking for the perfect man? What if you never find him? Are you going to spend the rest of your life alone?'

The doorbell rang sharply and they both started. The noise went on, getting louder, more peremptory.

'Is that *him*? It sounds like him,' Tom said angrily. 'I'll deal with this. You stay here.'

'No, Tom,' she anxiously said, trying to stop him, but he was already on his way to the front door like an advancing army, bristling with war-like intent. Pippa ran after him, caught up just as he yanked the door open and glared at Randal standing outside.

'Clear off. You're not wanted. By either of us!' Tom barked.

'Pippa can talk for herself. She doesn't need you talking for her!' Randal drawled with an infuriating look of superiority.

'She's engaged to me!'

'That doesn't make her a deaf mute! Even if you'd like her to be one!'

'How dare you?' fumed Tom.

Pippa suddenly sensed they had an audience; across the road a curtain twitched, eyes peered at them, and a woman coming down the road had halted to stare, fascinated.

Angrily, Pippa hissed. 'Come inside. People are watching!'

'Not until this fellow has left!' Tom said with a sullen glare at Randal.

'I'm not going anywhere.' Randal shrugged.

Flushed and distressed, Pippa pulled Tom back inside the cottage and Randal coolly followed, closing the front door behind him.

'Tell him to go away,' Tom urged, giving her that pleading look again, making her feel guilty and very sorry for him. 'What's he doing here, anyway? You said you were never going to see him again, so why's he here?'

Randal gave her a narrowed, dangerous look. 'Did you say that? Did he ask you to promise not to see me again? And did you agree?'

'I asked you not to come here,' she reminded him, chin lifted and green eyes angry.

'And now I see why,' he said through his teeth. 'You'd arranged to meet him here and I would have been very much *de trop*.'

'No! I hadn't arranged to meet him. He arrived out of the blue.'

'And talked you into going ahead with the wedding? He's got your lipstick on his mouth, so don't tell me he hasn't been kissing you!'

'What if I have? It's no business of yours!' erupted Tom. 'Our wedding is no business of yours. You aren't wanted here; she just told you. You see? I knew how she felt. She's no deaf mute. She's saying what I said she would say. So, why don't you just clear off? And don't come back.'

'I'll do whatever I damned well please!' Randal bit out.

Pippa's mouth went dry; she had never seen him look so angry. He scared her.

But she wouldn't let him see that; she pushed between him and Tom, staring angrily at Randal.

'Go away! I told you not to come here, and I meant it. And stop threatening Tom. Or I'll hit you with the nearest heavy object!'

He looked down at her, his face softening, relaxing, his mouth curling at the edges with amusement and his grey eyes dancing.

'I'm really scared!'

'I mean it!'

He held his hands up, palms towards her. 'Okay, okay, I'll be good. Promise, miss.'

She studied his features, hoping he meant it, but not assured by the amused mockery in his eyes, then turned to Tom. 'I think you'd better go now, Tom.'

Tom was still in a belligerent mood. 'Why should I leave? Tell him to go.'

'I will,' she told him firmly. 'But first I want you to go. I don't want you both leaving at the same time.

I don't want a fight starting up outside the cottage; the neighbours have had enough excitement for today. Once you've driven off, he can go.'

'Tell him to go first, then I'll leave. Why should I be the first to go?' Tom stubbornly said.

She put her hand on his arm, her eyes pleading. 'Don't be difficult, Tom, don't go on arguing. Just leave, please.'

He hesitated, clearly very reluctant to climb down, especially in front of Randal, but eventually shrugged. 'Oh, very well, but only for you.' Averting his eyes from Randal, he marched out of the room towards the front door. Pippa followed, ruefully wondering why men were always so obsessed with their pride, their sense of themselves.

She had the strong feeling that Tom was more concerned with defeating Randal than he was with her.

Tom opened the front door, then paused, looked at her. 'Will you be staying on here, in the cottage?'

'No. I'm going to sell it. I'll contact an estate agent later today, or tomorrow.'

'Don't do that. I'll buy it. You know I've always loved it. It will save you the agent's percentage to sell it direct to me.'

She was taken aback. 'Are you sure you really want to live here?'

'Certain. I'll get the house valued to make sure I'm paying the market price; I don't want you to feel I'm cheating you. Or you can get an agent to value it, if you prefer. Once we've agreed the price, we can complete the deal through our solicitors.'

Slowly, she nodded. 'Okay, Tom. You have the house valued. I trust you. Get in touch with someone. He can ring me to make an appointment to view the cottage.' She smiled at him. 'It will save me a lot of money to cut out an agent.'

He nodded, then shot a look past her into the hall. 'Are you sure you can deal with him? I'll sit in my car, if you like, until he goes.'

'There's no need, Tom. I'll be okay.'

He shrugged, smoothing down his fair hair. 'Very well, if you're sure. But don't let him talk you into seeing him again.'

'I won't, don't worry.'

Tom bent and kissed her lightly on her lips, said huskily, 'I'm going to miss you.' Then he walked away, got into his car, and drove off.

Sighing, Pippa slowly closed the front door and turned back, starting as she found Randal only a few feet behind her, his graceful body leaning against the wall in a casual manner which did not, disguise his poised capacity to be difficult.

'Were you eavesdropping?' she angrily demanded.

He raised one brow mockingly. 'I wanted to make sure he left without making any more trouble.'

'It was you who made the trouble!' She opened the front door again. 'Now, will you go, please?'

He sauntered back towards the kitchen, saying over his shoulder, 'Not yet.'

She let the door slam again and ran after him. 'I don't want you here! We've got nothing to say to each other. We've said it all.'

He swung, and the tension in his long, powerful body sent her heart into her throat. 'I haven't. Why did you let him kiss you?'

'I didn't let him. It just happened! But it's not your business, anyway.'

'Oh, yes, it is,' he said, and she looked up again

to find his grey eyes focused on her mouth with an intensity that made her pulses race.

She didn't want to respond like that. She wanted him to go away and leave her alone. But when he looked at her with such desire she felt her own passion leap up to meet his, and that terrified her.

'Leave me alone!' she whispered, her heart beating worryingly fast.

He pushed the chair aside and took her shoulders in his strong, supple hands. 'You belong to me, Pippa, you know that, even though you keep trying to pretend you don't. From the minute we met we both knew we were meant for each other. If I'd been free then, we'd have been together all these years, but by bad luck I wasn't free, so you ran away, and you're still running. Why?'

'I told you. You've ruined my life twice—I'm not going to let you do it again!'

'You love me,' he whispered, his hand going down to her waist, pulling her closer. 'I love you, too. Stop wasting any more of our time.' His cheek descended against her face, their skin brushing softly. She wanted to resist, push him away, but she was paralysed, her whole being intent on her awareness of his heart beating against her own, his arm round her waist, his thigh pressing into hers, his mouth sliding over her cheek to her mouth. However hard she tried, she could not fight his physical power over her.

His kiss parted her lips. The warm tip of his tongue slid through into her mouth, his other hand went up the back of her head and cradled it, his fingers in her hair, softly pulling her head back as his kiss drove into her.

'No, don't,' she muttered under that fierce, possessive mouth.

He kissed her harder, more demandingly, and she groaned, her lips trembling, burning. Eyes shut, she clung to him in spite of her warning brain, in spite of all her reasons for fighting him off. It was the same every time—the instant he touched her she melted like candle wax in his hands.

Suddenly, she was floating, like a leaf in the wind. She fought to force her eyes open, dazedly looked up at him, her body still shuddering with pleasure. He had picked her up bodily and was carrying her in his arms, a hand under her legs, the other around her shoulders.

'What...what are you doing?' she whispered, but he didn't answer.

She found out what his intentions were a second later as he lowered her to the couch in the sitting room. Angrily, she tried to get up again, but he was beside her, fencing her in, a little heap of cushions behind her and his long, lean body stretching out in front.

'I hate you!' she breathed, trembling with an explosive mixture of rage and helpless desire. He was dangerously close, their bodies touching at every point from her shoulders to her feet, and she was on fire, wanting him so much it felt like dying. Yet at the same time a warning voice inside her head told her it was dangerous, lethal; he would only hurt her again. She must not let herself surrender.

'Do you, Pippa?' he asked silkily, smiling as he stared down into her bitter green eyes.

'Yes! I hate the sight of you,' she insisted, staring back at him with such fixed intensity that for a moment she wasn't even conscious of what his lean fingers were doing, until she abruptly realised he had pushed up her turquoise sweater and undone her bra, and begun stroking and caressing her naked breasts.

Her heart thudded against her ribcage; she gasped, 'No! Stop that!'

Randal's head came down; his lips opened on one of her hot, swollen nipples, drew it inside the moist warmth of his mouth, and sucked.

Pippa moaned, pushing at his head, but it was immovable and she was helpless in the grip of pleasure. Her body was arching towards his, even while she tried to push him off. She despised herself for finding it impossible to resist him, but the ecstasy of his sucking mouth made her ache and shudder. She wanted him badly, badly. It would be so easy to give in, open her body to him and hold him inside herself, merge with him until they were one person, even if it was just for a few moments.

But the instant satisfaction he could give her wouldn't last; she would come out of it and have to face herself afterwards. This need she felt was purely physical, sheer sensuality, a wild, beating urge deep in her body. Her mind warned her not to give in to it.

'I'm not sleeping with you!' she broke out, struggling.

His head lifted, his face darkly flushed, his eyes sensuous, drowsy. A wry smile curled his mouth. 'Stop fighting the way you feel, Pippa. You want me to make love to you, even if you're determined to insist you don't.'

He looked down at her body again, bent and ran the tip of his warm tongue softly over the nipple he had been sucking, and she couldn't keep back a cry of intense pleasure.

'You see?' he said. 'You want it, just as much as I do. What I don't understand is why you keep protesting that you don't.'

CHAPTER SEVEN

'YES, okay,' she broke out hoarsely. 'I go out of my head when you make love to me. I don't deny it.' Angrily, she saw him smile, his grey eyes glittering in triumph, and went on in a hurry, 'But I still don't want to get involved with you again. Last time I got hurt and I don't want to get hurt again. I keep telling you that. Why can't you get the point?'

He grimaced impatiently. 'Not again! We keep having the same circular argument! But if you insist, we'll go round again. Sooner or later maybe I'll make you listen. Four years ago, I was married. Now I'm free. We both know that. I'm in love with you, I want you, you just admitted you feel the same—so where's the problem?'

While he was talking in that brusque, impatient tone, she was discreetly clipping her bra together again, pulling down her sweater, smoothing her tangled chestnut hair. When he'd finished, she got up in a quick movement, before he could stop her, walked to the window, stood there with her back to him, speaking quietly. 'The problem is simple, Randal. I don't want to get hurt again. You know I was abandoned as a child—four years ago I felt I was being dumped again, when you chose your marriage and your child over me.'

He started to protest. 'For heaven's sake! What else could I do? He was only little; I couldn't walk out on him...'

She interrupted. 'Randal, listen! I'm not saying you were wrong. I understand. Your little boy needed you and had the right to expect that you would be there for him, protect him, make sure he was happy.'

'I'm his father; I had to look after him. Renata was far too selfish to bother about a child, even her own. All she wanted was to have a good time, and looking after a little boy didn't come into her scheme of things.'

'I know Johnny needed you to take care of him. I see that. I know you had no real choice. You felt you had to stay with your wife for his sake. But that doesn't change the fact that I felt you didn't really care about me. And, however good your reasons, I want a man who'll really care about me.'

He got up from the couch impatiently, his voice rising. 'Of course I cared about you, Pippa! How can you think I didn't? It was a terrible choice I was forced to make! Do you think I found it easy? I agonised over it for a long time.'

She swung round to face him, her face pale and grave. 'I just said, I know why you had to put your son first. But understanding doesn't alter anything. When it came to it, you chose your marriage and your child, not me, and I know you always would.'

He ran his hands through his hair in restless frustration. 'I had to then! What else could I do? You keep saying you understand, but do you? I had to choose Johnny four years ago, but it's different now. Everything's sorted. My marriage is legally over. Johnny's at boarding school. I've had a private detective looking for you ever since my divorce was finalised. You've been on my mind all this time. I love you, Pippa, and now we can get married. There's nothing in the way of us being together.'

'There's me, Randal.'

He stopped a few feet away and stared at her, eyes glittering, sharp, probing her face. 'What does that mean?'

'I won't let it happen to me again. I know now that you'll always put your son first and me second.'

'Pippa, it isn't a contest. You're being ridiculous! You sound as if you're jealous of Johnny, jealous of a little boy; that's crazy.'

'No, of course not. I'm not jealous of him. But I'm still afraid of getting hurt. You say you love me, but I'd never feel I was really important in your life.'

'Pippa…' He reached for her and she backed away, shaking her head.

'No! Please go, Randal, don't drag this out. I'm serious. I mean what I say, and it won't make any difference in the long run for you to make love to me. We both know I'd find it hard to say no at the time, but afterwards I'd still feel the same. I got hurt last time; I don't want to be hurt again. I've thought long and hard about this. There's no future for us.'

He raked back his tousled hair, grimly staring at her. 'I don't accept that! You're making a stupid fuss about nothing.'

She shrugged. 'If you think that, you just aren't listening or trying to understand. There's no point in talking. I'm not going to change my mind and you're refusing to see my point of view.'

'Okay, I'll leave—but you promised to come with me to see Johnny. Will you at least keep your word about that?'

She made a weary gesture. 'What good would it

do? I'm not going to be part of your life. There's no point in my meeting him.'

Randal was as serious as she was now, his grey eyes level and silvery, like cooling metal, hardening and losing colour as if all the passion had drained out of him, leaving him icy cold. 'I think there is. I'd like him to know you. The two of you matter more to me than anyone else in my life. I want you to know each other.'

She bit her lower lip, frowning. 'Why? What's the point?'

'I just told you. I want you to meet, even if it's only once. And you promised you would. A few hours of your time, that's all I'm asking you—surely you can spare a few hours?'

Pippa groaned. 'Why are you so obstinate. You never give up, do you?'

He shook his head. 'Not when something really matters to me.'

She sighed deeply, thinking. 'Oh, very well, I'll come, just once. And then…that's it, okay? You understand? You accept that I do not want to see you ever again after that?'

He nodded. 'I hear what you say. I'll pick you up on Friday, mid-morning, around eleven. Bring a change of clothes and a nightie. We'll be spending the weekend at a hotel.'

'Oh, will we?' she bit out, body tensing in immediate alarm and distrust.

He caught her quick sideways, suspicious look and laughed in light mockery. 'Oh, don't worry, I'm not planning a seduction scene. Johnny will be sharing my room; you'll have one of your own. You'll be quite safe.'

She had never been safe with him; since the beginning he had made her desperately happy, then bitterly unhappy, and she was determined never to let him risk her happiness again. Next time she fell in love she wanted it to be with someone who loved her the way she needed to be loved, who put her first.

She walked away from him to the front door, opened it. Randal came after her, looked down at her searchingly. 'By the way, did I hear you agreeing to sell this cottage to Tom?'

'I knew you were eavesdropping! You have no shame at all, do you? When you're after your own way you'll do anything to get it.' She shrugged contemptuously. 'But, yes, Tom asked me to sell it directly to him instead of putting it on the market. We were going to live here together, you know, once we were married; he likes the cottage.'

'I hope you're going to have it professionally valued!'

'Of course, but it's going to make selling it much easier. It will save me the ten per cent the agent would charge, and I trust Tom.'

'I can't say I do!' Randal snorted.

'You don't know him! He's a good man.'

'So he isn't buying the cottage just to stay in constant contact with you?'

She resented the dry, ironic note in his voice. 'No, certainly not. He's buying it because he loves it, he always has—and after all, I was going to sell it anyway. The sale will be handled through our solicitors; we won't need to be in contact.

'I was jealous,' he coolly retorted. 'He had your lipstick on his mouth, it was obvious he'd been kissing you, and I was jealous.'

She felt hot colour burn along her throat and face, and looked down, taken aback. The fierceness of his voice made her melt internally, made her legs weak.

He watched her briefly, his face unreadable, then said, 'See you on Friday.'

He walked down the short drive, got into his car and drove off. Pippa watched him vanish, then went in and shut the front door before going upstairs to have a cooling shower and put on a thin cotton shirt and a pair of cream linen trousers. Love was altogether too exhausting. She could not bear many more scenes like that. Fighting Randal had left scars on her heart and mind. She felt mauled, as if she had been in a cage with a tiger and barely escaped with her life.

She sat down to write her letter of resignation to the insurance company. Before she started looking for another job, it might be a good idea to have a long holiday. She felt she needed one.

She spent the warm spring afternoon in her garden, mowing the lawn, pruning and weeding; it was a peaceful occupation, and she didn't need to think too hard, but her body used up a lot of the buzzing energy inside her. The weather stayed fine and bright; it was pleasant in the sun. By the time she had eaten a salad and watched TV for an hour or so she was tired enough to go to bed and sleep without difficulty, keeping thoughts of Randal at bay when she was awake but finding him invading her dreams when she slept.

On Thursday Tom came round with a surveyor to price the cottage. While the man wandered around, measuring rooms and testing various parts of the building for signs of woodworm or damp, or other problems, Pippa and Tom sat outside in the garden with coffee and biscuits.

'You should make quite a bit of money on the deal,' Tom said in his calm, practical way. 'You got the place very cheaply and you did the bulk of the redecoration yourself so you didn't really spend too much on it. It was a very good investment. You'll finish up with a considerable profit. Will you buy another place at once, or invest the money and rent somewhere for the moment?'

'First I've decided to have a holiday.' That reminded her of something she had forgotten. 'Did you manage to cancel the honeymoon?'

'It was far too late for that. I've decided to go alone.'

She bit her lip. 'Oh. I'm sorry, Tom...'

'I'm sure I'll enjoy it. I was due a holiday anyway. Where were you thinking of going?'

'I haven't thought about it yet. When I come back, though, I'll have to get another job, then I'll see what property values are like wherever I move. I sent my resignation in, by the way. They should have it by now.'

Tom nodded, staring at two robins squabbling over some nesting material, a few scraps of twine Pippa had used to tie up lupins months ago, in the summer. They had frayed and broken, were hanging loose; the robins each had hold of one of them and were pulling and squawking crossly at each other.

'What about...him? Are you seeing him? Going on holiday with him?'

She sighed. 'Tom, don't keep asking about Randal, please. I don't want to talk about him.' She shaded her eyes to look up at the sky. 'It's such a lovely morning; don't waste it.'

Tom looked sulky, then said, 'What will you do with your wedding dress? Keep it for next time? When you marry him?'

She winced at the sting of the question. She couldn't blame him for feeling bitter, though. She hadn't broken Tom's heart, she didn't think he was madly in love with her, but she had damaged his ego, his sense of himself, and to the sort of man Tom was that would be very painful. His dignity was very important to him.

'I've talked to the dressmaker and paid her. I'll put the dress away for the moment.' She put a hand on his arm tentatively. 'I'm sorry, Tom. I've made a mess of your life, I know that, but I never intended to. It was just bad luck that we had that crash and I met...him...again. But although it was bad luck in one way, I do think it was just as well in another. How could we have been happy when I didn't really love you the way you should be loved? Sooner or later you would have realised something was missing and then it would have been ten times worse for both of us.'

He grunted, head turned away. She couldn't tell what he was thinking from the grim profile which was all she could see.

'You'll meet someone else, Tom,' she offered uncertainly. 'And this time it will be love on both sides.'

The surveyor, a thin young man with horn-rimmed spectacles and a very serious expression, came out to join them, looking around the garden. 'Very pretty out here, isn't it? This is a really charming property, in fact. I'll have to measure the land too, before we

go. But you've done a very good job with the cottage.
I gather it was in a pretty poor condition when you
bought it, and you did most of the decorating yourself?'

'All of it, apart from the retiling of the roof and
the plumbing. I even put in most of the kitchen myself, modernised it all. The old man who lived here
hadn't touched the place for years and years.'

'Well, I'm impressed. You're very clever.'

'Thank you. Coffee?' She picked up the vacuum
jug of coffee; it would still be hot.

'Black, no sugar,' he said, smiling at her, his blue
eyes twinkling behind the heavy spectacles. 'Do you
do the garden yourself, too?'

'Mostly, yes. I can't afford to pay people to do
things for me. I enjoy gardening, anyway. In fact, I
like doing things well; it gives me a buzz.'

He sipped his coffee. 'I know what you mean. I
suppose most of us like doing things well. And you
make good coffee, by the way.'

She laughed. 'Thanks.'

Tom shifted impatiently in his chair, irritated by
this light-hearted conversation. 'Have you talked to
your solicitor yet, Pippa? About selling the cottage?'

'I alerted him to the prospect. He didn't seem to
foresee any problems.'

'Good. I expect you want to finalise the deal as
soon as possible. I've put my own place on the market, but if it doesn't sell at once the firm will help me
with a temporary mortgage on the cottage.'

'That will be helpful and should speed the deal.'

The surveyor finished his coffee and got up. 'I'll
get on with measuring the garden and the rest of the

area on which the cottage stands, then I can draw up a map to go with the deeds.'

As he walked away Tom looked at his watch. 'Half past eleven. Nearly lunchtime. Will you have lunch with me, Pippa?'

'Sorry, I'm too busy,' she quickly said. The sooner she stopped seeing Tom the better, for both of them. There was no point whatever in continuing to see him. His restless impatience with the surveyor just now made it obvious that he did not see her in any simply friendly light. He hadn't yet cut the strings that had bound them together. If he didn't set eyes on her for months, he would finally forget they had ever been about to marry, especially as she was quite certain he was not in love with her. Theirs had been an affair of proximity. Tom had wanted to marry her because she was the sort of wife he had always meant to pick. She was competent, sensible, good with money and a home-maker—he had felt he could trust her.

Now they both knew he had been wrong. She hadn't been the wife for him, any more than he was the man for her. Tom was possessive, but he was not passionate; that was why he had been happy to wait to sleep with her. Pippa had been forced to realise that she was very definitely passionate—she burned with desire whenever Randal touched her. She wanted to feel that way about the man she did eventually marry.

But it would not be Randal himself. He didn't love her enough. He loved his child more, and although she admired him for his fidelity to the little boy it still hurt her feelings.

The truth was, Randal didn't love her the way she needed to be loved. That was the root reason why she

would not marry him. She wanted a man who would
love her more than anyone else in his life, always put
her first. The emptiness and loneliness of her childhood had left her aching. How often she had envied
friends their homes, their parents, brothers and sis-
ters—the affection and caring of those they lived
with.

How often she had wished she had those things,
too. She had always yearned for love, to be the centre
of somebody's world, to know she was beloved and
cherished. She would never have that with Randal.
Oh, she believed him when he said he loved her, she
knew he desired her, but the strong, protective love
she had hungered for as a child would never come to
her from Randal. He gave that to his son, which was
only natural.

When Tom and the surveyor had left she sat on in
the sunshine, facing facts about herself. It was childish and immature, no doubt, to want to come first with
Randal—she knew people would see it that way, and
maybe they were right, but she couldn't help her own
instinctive reactions. She had dreamt for too long of
finding someone who would love her the way she
needed to be loved. She couldn't abandon her dream
now.

The following morning she was up early, having
slept badly. First, she packed a light weekend case,
taking the bare minimum of clothes.

Then she had a shower before getting dressed in a
simple green silk tunic which cut off just above her
knee. With it she wore white high-heeled sandals and
carried a white shoulder bag. The impression left by
her reflection in her dressing table was one of cool
elegance. She was satisfied by that. The last thing she

wanted was to encourage Randal to think she might
be an easy target.

She forced herself to eat some fruit and a slice of
toast, then filled in the time before Randal arrived by
checking that the cottage was scrupulously tidy, locking all the windows and doors apart from the front
door. As she finished Randal drove up in his gleaming
sports car.

Pippa's heart missed a beat, she suddenly couldn't
breathe, but somehow she managed to pick up her
weekend case and go out to meet him, locking the
cottage door behind her. Randal got out of his car and
took her case, put it in the boot, while, legs weak
under her, she walked round to the passenger door
and got into the front seat.

Randal slid in beside her, stretched those long, long
legs of his, and started the engine again. She glanced
sidelong at his lightweight pale blue linen jacket, the
even paler trousers, exquisitely tailored, the smooth
dark blue leather shoes which shrieked money.
Randal was a luxury item from head to foot; he
looked gorgeous. She looked at the supple, powerful
hands on the wheel and had a heart-stopping flash of
memory; those hands touching her as they had on the
couch in the cottage, stroking her breasts while his
mouth moved possessively on her bare skin.

She wrenched her gaze away and stared fixedly out
of the window, shuddering.

She mustn't let herself remember. She had to get
over him, stop wanting him, stop loving him.

But how did she do that when every bone in her
body melted at the thought of being in his arms?

She had to make herself think about something else.

'How long will it take to reach this school?' She tried to sound calm and relaxed, hard though it was when she was so deeply conscious of being alone with him in this tiny space, their shoulders, their legs only inches apart.

'An hour and a half. I've said we'll pick up Johnny for lunch. I booked a table at the hotel; it isn't far from the school, and the cooking is extremely good. They have a top-class chef.'

'Does Johnny know I'm coming with you?'

'Yes, I talked to him on the phone last night. He was very excited about spending the weekend out of school—although he loves the school, going away is a stimulating experience for him. There's a riding stable near the hotel; he wants to spend a couple of hours there tomorrow. Would you like to ride?'

'Well, I have ridden a horse a few times, Tom thought it would be fun to go—but I'm strictly a beginner and I haven't brought any suitable clothes. I don't have any jodhpurs or boots or a hard hat, and it's dangerous to ride without a hat, at least.'

'Maybe they hire the gear out?'

'You know the place, I suppose. You've been there before with your son? Do they?'

'I've no idea, I've never asked, but if we can hire what you need do you want to ride?'

'It could be fun—are you going to ride?'

'I will, if you will. There's a qualified riding instructor who can look after Johnny, if we don't ride, but I'd like to go just to keep an eye on him.'

'And you have got the right gear with you?'

He nodded. 'After Johnny said he wanted to ride, I looked out some boots and jodhpurs, and I found a rather old hat which will do. There was no point in

ringing you though, because the shops were shut by
then, and I thought the stable might be able to find
you some gear.'

'Well, if they don't hire clothes I'll watch. Don't
worry about me.' She leaned back in her seat, watching the green English countryside flash past.

As they turned a corner another car tore towards
them at a dangerous speed and Randal braked to
avoid a crash, skewing his car closer to the hedge, as
he had that night he and Tom crashed.

The other car screeched past. Randal came to a full
stop, the bonnet of the sports car mere inches from
the hedge. Silence fell on them like the dust of this
quiet, narrow country lane.

Pippa only then realised that she had screamed. The
echo of her cry of fear went on and on inside her
head, and beside her she heard Randal angrily swear-
ing.

After a minute, he turned towards her, releasing his
seat belt, his face full of concern.

'Are you okay? I'm sorry about that. He was doing
about eighty miles an hour—we're lucky I wasn't
driving fast myself and we came out of it unscathed.'

She laughed unsteadily, tears of fear and wild humour in her green eyes. '*Déjà vu*. That was pure *déjà
vu*. Just like the night you and Tom crashed into each
other.'

He smiled wryly. 'I suppose it was. My heart is
going like a steamhammer. Feel it.'

He took her hand and carried it to his chest, laid
in on his shirt above where his heart beat violently.
The warmth of his body lay under her palm; she
pressed down on it, wanting desperately to undo his
blue shirt and feel his skin against hers.

Randal watched her face closely and must have read the leap of hunger in her eyes because he suddenly leant over, his body above hers, coming down on her, holding her down. She knew she should push him away, refuse to let him kiss her, but the shock of the near accident was still inside her; she felt reckless, abandoned. She met his mouth with passion, her lips parting. His hands caressed her, and she felt desire tear through her like a hurricane, destroying everything in its path.

If they had not been sitting in a car at that moment, heaven knew what might have happened next, but they were parked on a public road and visible to anyone driving past. They could not go too far.

Randal groaned, slowly lifting his mouth. 'I would kill to have you now. Do you know what you do to me?'

Dazedly she lay there, eyes half closed, breathing thickly. She knew what he did to her—did he feel like this?

Her senses rioted: heart beating dangerously fast, pulses throbbing with fever, heat burning deep inside her. She hadn't wanted him to stop, had needed him to go on, to take her, satisfy this terrible need.

'We'd better get on or we'll be late arriving at the school, and even later for lunch,' Randal said, running a hand over his deeply flushed face. 'Sit up, Pippa. Stop tempting me.'

He clipped his seat belt together, started the engine again and slowly moved off, and she closed her eyes, fighting to get back to normal.

The rest of the drive was uneventful; they didn't talk any more. She pretended to be asleep and, indeed, did doze a little, drifting in and out of daydreams, fragments of memory, of him kissing her, touching her.

They reached the school just as many other cars were leaving, loaded with boys being taken off for the weekend by their parents. Randal parked on the wide gravel driveway, left her in her seat and walked into the school to find his son.

Pippa curiously gazed up at the building, built rather like a Scottish castle, with four storeys of stone walls draped with Virginia creeper, rows of arched windows and, at each end, turreted towers. She hoped it had central heating or it must be an icebox in winter.

A few minutes later Randal returned with his son, who was carrying in one hand a leather overnight bag. Johnny was taller than she had expected, a healthy-looking boy with his father's dark hair and slim build, but as they came closer she saw that he had sensitive features, wide blue eyes, a fine nose and wide mouth, a mobile face that reflected his emotions as he talked to his father.

She slid out of her seat to greet him, smiling.

'Johnny, this is Pippa,' Randal told him, taking his overnight bag and putting it into the boot of the car, and the boy held out his hand, staring at her.

'Hello.'

'Hi, Johnny,' she said, holding his small, slim fingers warmly. How much did he take after his mother? Physically he was very like Randal, but what about his nature, his personality? Was that inherited from Randal, too, or from his mother?

'We have to hurry,' Randal told them. 'We mustn't be late for lunch at the hotel. Hop in, Johnny.'

They drove off a moment later and were soon at

the hotel, a white Georgian building in spacious gardens. Randal manoeuvred his way through the arched gateway into the car park behind the hotel.

'This was once a coaching inn, in the eighteenth century,' he told her and Johnny. 'The coaches came through that arch and their horses were stabled overnight in those boxes, groomed, fed and watered, to rest until early next morning.'

The old stables had been painted pristine white and were used as outbuildings. Hanging baskets of flowers swung along the walls, spilling geraniums and nasturtiums, pink and white and vivid orange, giving colour to the ancient stone-cobbled floor. They all got out. Randal carried their bags through a door marked 'Reception'; Pippa and Johnny followed him into the low-ceilinged lobby and found him signing them all in while a pretty receptionist watched him, smiling.

A porter collected their luggage, to take it to their rooms, while they walked through the hotel to the dining room for lunch.

As the head waiter showed them to their table Johnny gave a little gasp and stopped dead, staring across the room at another table where a ravishing blonde was half rising, staring too.

'Mummy!'

Pippa's heart burned over in sick dismay.

CHAPTER EIGHT

So THAT was Renata, Randal's ex-wife! And she was every bit as beautiful as everyone had ever said she was. Her figure was full and curvy, high, beautifully shaped breasts emphasised by the lilac shirt she wore, the lapels open and deep, revealing the smooth golden flesh, a trim waist, slim hips and long, long legs in white, tight-fitting jeans. Her hair was the colour of summer corn, ripe and golden, falling in rich waves around her lovely face.

Every man in the place was staring avidly, coveting her. Pippa gave Randal a quick, searching look, and found him staring too.

He must have been in love with her once. Perhaps he still was under his talk of hating her? It wouldn't be surprising. Pippa knew she, herself, was attractive, but she had no illusions. She couldn't hold a candle to Renata. The other woman was one of the best-looking women she had ever seen.

She was smiling now, at her son, and Johnny ran to her, was gathered up in her open arms and kissed.

'Surprise, surprise!' she cooed at him.

Randal walked over there, too, as if drawn by invisible ropes, said curtly, 'Why didn't you let us know you were coming?'

'I did say I'd try, didn't I? But I wasn't sure I'd make it. I didn't want to disappoint him if I couldn't get here.' Still holding her son's hand, she smiled up at Randal lazily, her blue eyes sultry. 'How are you, Randal? You look terrific.'

'I'm fine.' Randal shot a glance at the man seated at the table, gave him an unfriendly nod. 'Hello, Alex.'

'Hi, how're you?' the other man drawled in a strong Australian accent. He was tall, bronzed, blond, with a clean-cut profile, and wore a tan linen suit, jacket open to show a lemon shirt.

'Fine thanks.' Randal held his hand out to his son. 'But we'd better have our lunch now—see you later, no doubt. We're staying here. Are you?'

'For tonight, at least,' Renata said. 'Maybe we could have dinner?' She glanced past Randal at where Pippa was standing beside their table. 'Is that your girlfriend? You didn't say there was someone special. We must meet her—could we make up a foursome tonight?' Her gaze coolly slipped over Pippa in her simple green silk tunic, one pencilled brow lifting in silent, unfavourable comment. 'Pretty,' she murmured in tones that made it clear she did not really think Pippa was anything of the kind, and Pippa stiffened in resentment. Who did she think she was?

'Give us a ring later,' Randal said remotely, walking away, bringing Johnny with him.

As the little boy sat down he looked at Pippa and said, 'That's my mummy.'

'Yes,' Pippa said with a forced, bright smile, picking up the menu and pretending to study it with interest.

Johnny copied her, following the words with his finger.

'Can I have this melon filled with fresh fruit?' he

asked his father. 'Sorbet's a kind of ice cream, isn't it?'

'Yes, and this is raspberry sorbet. Good choice. I think I'll have the same.'

'Steak with peaches? That sounds nice. I never ate steak with fruit before.'

'Excellent,' Randal said, as if not quite listening. His forehead was lined; he looked abstracted.

Watching him from behind lowered lashes, Pippa caught the frowning look he threw across the room at his wife and wished she knew precisely what was going on inside his head. Clearly it had thrown him to see Renata here—but just what sort of shock had it been? There was a streak of dark red across his strong cheekbones, a little tic under one eye. Randal was trying to seem calm and in control, but obviously he was nothing of the kind.

The waiter came and took their order. She had melon, too, with fruit and the raspberry sorbet, followed by halibut in a light orange sauce.

Johnny talked excitedly about an adventure trip he had been taken on by the school the previous week. 'We camped in the woods and did canoeing and climbed trees—I climbed to the top of one, and I didn't fall out, but Jamie fell and broke his wrist so he can't do games or swim and can only write one-handed. And we ran races. I got a blister as big as this...' He measured an improbable size with his fingers. 'It burst and pink stuff came out...'

'Thank you, very interesting, but no medical details while we're eating,' his father said. 'I'm glad you had a great time. But be careful climbing trees. You don't want to break your wrist, do you?'

'No. Jamie screamed,' Johnny said thoughtfully.

'Screamed and screamed. And now he's got plaster on his wrist and can't do anything. We all wrote our names on the plaster and drew cartoons.'

As they were drinking their coffee Renata and the blond Australian came past and paused. She gave a dazzling smile to Randal and purred, 'We'd like to take Johnny for a drive to have tea somewhere— would that be okay? It's ages since I saw him. Please, Randal?'

Randal considered her dispassionately, his grey eyes remote, then looked at his son. 'Up to you, Johnny. Do you want to go for a drive with Mummy and Alex?'

Pippa read his uneasy hesitation, the uncertainty in his eyes. He sneaked a look at the blond golf champion. Was Alex a hero to him? wondered Pippa as he slowly said, 'Well, okay, then, if you don't mind, Dad.'

'Whatever you want to do is okay with me, Johnny,' Randal reassured firmly, and the boy's face lightened.

'Come on,' Renata said, offering her hand, and he got up from the table and went with her. Over her shoulder she said to Randal, 'See you at dinner.'

When they had gone Randal let out a long, rough sigh. 'There wasn't any choice, was there? I couldn't refuse to let him go while he was there, listening. I don't want him blaming me because he never sees her.'

'I'm sure he wouldn't. You seem to have a great relationship, the two of you.'

He smiled at her. 'Do you think so? Well, I hope so. It isn't that I want to stop her seeing him—I wish she visited him more often—but Renata is given to arbitrary fits of spite. She might suddenly decide to take off with him, not bring him back—only to get bored with the game after a day or two and dump him, and Johnny could get hurt.'

Dryly, Pippa said, 'I don't think she'll run off with him. I think she's looking forward to playing a very different game tonight, at dinner.'

He gave her a shrewd, sharp look. 'What are you talking about?'

Pippa lifted a shoulder in a shrug. 'She may enjoy having a succession of men, but I got the impression she was still interested in you. Maybe she's the type to want to keep any man she's owned once on a leash, and she resents the fact that you got away.'

'Do you think so?' he asked, finishing his coffee.

Pippa did not add that she also suspected that his ex-wife had not been pleased to see him with another woman, especially one who was a good ten years younger.

'If you're ready, shall we check out our rooms and unpack?' he suggested, rising, and she agreed, following him out to the reception area. They collected their keys and took the lift upstairs to the first floor.

Pippa let herself into her own room; Randal stood at the door, staring round, frowning. The room was small but comfortable, with a single bed. On a luggage rack against the wall stood Johnny's overnight bag.

'They obviously thought Johnny was going to be using this room,' Pippa said, seeing a connecting door open, leading into another room.

Randal walked over there and went through into what turned out to be a sitting room. Pippa followed him across that into a third room, a spacious double bedroom with twin beds covered in blue silk brocade that matched the floor-length curtains. It was a charming room, with elegant eighteenth-century furniture. On the luggage rack were her suitcase and Randal's side by side.

She turned on him. 'You can't have made it clear that this room was for you and Johnny! They obviously thought you and I would be sharing this room, while the smaller room was for the child.'

'I didn't discuss the sleeping arrangements with the booking staff!' he said irritably. 'I just asked for a double suite and one single room. I'll ring down now and get you a better room.'

'No, don't bother—that room is fine.' She picked up her own case. 'I'll unpack. Would you collect Johnny's case and unpack for him?'

He took her case from her. 'Look, I'm sorry, Pippa. I didn't realise they would give you such a tiny room.'

'It doesn't matter; it's only for a couple of days.'

'You can use the sitting room as much as you like!' he offered in placation, carrying her case into her small bedroom.

She deliberately checked that there was a bolt on the inside of her bedroom door. 'Thank you.'

'Will you mind having dinner with Renata and Alex tonight?' he asked, removing Johnny's case from the luggage rack.

'No, why should I?' She put her case on the bed and unlocked it. Casually, she asked, 'You knew she was going to be here, didn't you? That's why you were so insistent I should come with you. I'm here as a trophy, to let her know you aren't still pining for her, you've already found another woman.'

His face filled with angry dark red, his eyes flashed. 'Don't be ridiculous! I told you, she rarely comes to see Johnny. I didn't expect to see her here!'

She did not believe him. Renata had said she had hinted that she might come, and Randal's pride, his male ego, had needed to convince his ex-wife that he had another woman, she needn't think he wasn't missing her.

Randal had been using her! Pippa felt jealousy and resentment burning deep inside, twisting like a knife in her entrails. All the way here, to the school, she had been wondering what might happen in this hotel, had been trying to work out how to keep Randal at bay, make certain he didn't try to share her bed once his son was asleep. She had been shaking with excitement and passion, too, because even while she was determined he should not make love to her she couldn't help wanting to be in his arms. It might be contradictory, irrational, crazy, but her body ached for his, however hard she tried to convince herself he was forbidden to her.

It hadn't even occurred to her that his ex-wife might turn up, or that Randal might have brought her along as a shield against Renata realising he still wanted her.

Because he must still want his ex-wife, or why would he have been so insistent about Pippa coming with him? She had seen his face at lunch, when he first glimpsed Renata across the room. She had seen his clenched features, the taut jawline, the glitter of his eyes. He still wanted Renata; he was jealous of the tall, tanned Australian golfer who, Pippa angrily decided, was a perfect match for the luscious blonde. They might have been made for each other, in fact, although Randal obviously wouldn't be too pleased if she told him so.

She started unpacking, walking to and fro, sliding clothes into drawers, hanging others up in the tiny wardrobe.

'Do you want me to unpack for Johnny, or will you?' she said without looking at him.

'You're jealous,' he said suddenly. 'You're jealous of Renata, aren't you?' He was at her elbow a second later, grabbing her by the shoulders and swinging her round to face him. 'Ever since we met again you've been trying to convince me you're indifferent, never want to see me again—but you're jealous of Renata, which proves you're nothing of the kind. You can't be jealous if you're indifferent.'

'I am not jealous!' she furiously snapped.

'Oh, yes, you are. I can see it in those big green eyes.' He held her away from him, gazing down into those eyes, his own flickering and gleaming, silvery stars.

'Pure imagination,' she flung back. 'Wishful thinking!'

His voice husky, he whispered, 'Believe me, Pippa, I never expected to see Renata here. I meant what I said—I wanted you and Johnny to get to know each other. And—' He broke off and she watched him suspiciously, trying to probe behind his features, see inside his head, read his mind.

'And what?' she insisted.

He hesitated. 'Nothing. I forget what I was going to say.'

'I don't believe you! Come on, you started to say something—finish it!'

He grimaced. 'Okay, but you won't like it! I was

going to say I wanted to spend the weekend with you!' He pulled her closer, his eyes eating her. 'You kept saying you didn't want to see me again, but I wasn't giving up. I meant to keep in contact with you.' One hand ran down her spine, over the soft silk of her dress, slowly, caressingly. When it reached the hem just above her knees, he pushed her dress upward, slid his hand up inside, between her thighs, fingertips sensuously brushing the inner secret heat, forcing a cry of excitement from her.

'You see? You want me,' he whispered, bending his head. His tongue-tip softly stroked her mouth. 'Close contact, that's what we both need.' He groaned, pulled her hard so that their bodies collided, touched, from shoulder to thigh. 'I need to touch you, make love to you.'

'No, don't! Stop that,' she broke out, trembling violently, her mouth hot from the mere touch of his tongue. She was aware of his body touching hers everywhere, the heat between them intolerable.

'And you need it, too, whether you'll admit it or not,' he muttered, one hand on her back, pressing her hard against him while he cradled her head in his spread fingers with the other, manoeuvring it into position so that he could kiss her.

She would rather die than admit anything of the kind, and she resisted his fierce, invading mouth, struggling so hard he shifted his hand from her spine to her waist and held her possessively, his hand just below her breast.

Her treacherous mouth had parted to admit him, her body clung hotly to his, but she still struggled—so furiously that the two of them swayed and toppled on to the bed, knocking her suitcase off, on to the floor, spilling her clothes in all directions.

'Let go, let go,' she cried, pushing at his wide shoulders.

Randal looked down at her, eyes half-open, smouldering, languorous, and her mouth went dry at the expression in those eyes.

He moved his hand to touch her breast and she drew a shaken breath. He slid an arm under her, lifting her, swiftly pulled her dress over her head, followed by her lacy white chemise and then her bra. She fought him uselessly, tried to stop him stripping her, but his deft fingers were too fast and certain. In seconds she was naked all but her brief white panties.

'You're so lovely,' Randal groaned, letting her slip back on to the bed and lying next to her. His grey eyes wandered freely over her nakedness, sensuously explored her breasts, moved downwards to her hips and thighs. He leaned over to kiss the pale flesh his eyes had just discovered. 'Beautiful,' he whispered.

Her eyes closed helplessly as his mouth heatedly caressed her breast, his hands stroking below, over her hips. Her tiny panties slid down; alarm shot through her as that last barrier went and she recognised that if she didn't stop him now he was going to take her and she would not be able to resist him.

She tried to struggle up, get off the bed, but he pulled her back so that her thighs fell open with him sliding between them. She wished desperately that it did not seem so natural to her to have them there, fitting with her like spoons in a drawer.

'I won't let you!' she gasped.

'Well, I won't force you,' he said thickly, staring down at her smooth bare flesh. 'But I need you,

Pippa, my God, I need you.' He kissed her again, deeply, passionately, and her eyes shut again, her lips moved in hot response, her body quivered. Every time he kissed her, touched her, he got the same reaction; she could not help it, even though she angrily despised herself for being so weak and foolish. Had her mind no control at all over her treacherous body, then?

Through the feverish clouds of her pleasure she suddenly realised Randal was taking off his jacket, then he was shrugging out of his shirt. He was stripping, she thought, appalled! As she realised what was happening she felt his legs kicking his trousers away.

Events were moving far too fast. She must stop it now, before it was too late!

But it was already too late. Randal was between her parted thighs and now he was naked, too, his bare skin brushing hers sensuously, his hands sliding beneath her, lifting her buttocks off the bed so that her knees fell apart.

'Randal, don't!' she groaned. 'I've never...I'm a... It would be my first time and I can't, not like this!'

'Sweet,' he whispered, kissing her. 'That's what I love about you, your innocence, your integrity and sense of self-respect. They are what make you the woman I adore.' His kiss deepened, took fire, until she drowned in it, forgetting everything else but him, her arms round his back, her body clinging to his.

'You're mine. You know you are,' Randal breathed against her parted, hungry lips. 'And I want you to be part of me, for ever.'

She wanted that, too, but she mustn't admit it. Between her thighs he moved in a slow, sensuous rhythm, and she moaned with pleasure, moving, too, opening to the seduction of that brushing contact. The pressure deepened, she felt him pushing into her, then a sharp pain. She gave a cry, 'You're hurting! Don't!' and tried to push him off, her palms flat on his naked chest.

Randal kissed her harder, groaning. 'Don't ask me to stop now, darling, not now, so close...'

Another pang of pain, fiercer, and then he was deep inside her, filling her, and she lay still, breathing wildly, feeling an intolerable ache of pain and satisfaction and desire. What was the point now of denying that she wanted this, had longed to merge with him, be part of him?

His mouth moved down to her breasts, sucked at her nipples, his hands cupping the warm, rounded flesh until she relaxed again, her pain forgotten, and a moment later he began moving again, his hot, hard flesh probing inside her, setting off jangling pulses in places where she had not known they existed, sending waves of ecstatic sensation through her entire body.

Over the next few minutes she almost lost consciousness, mind drowning in physical sensations, holding him, moving with him, mindlessly, sobbing in ecstasy. The next clear awareness she had was of lying still, limp and drained, with Randal collapsed on top of her, while tears ran down her face.

Suddenly he rolled off her. They were separate again and she felt cold and lonely, losing him.

'Don't cry,' he whispered. 'What is it? Did I really hurt you?'

She put her hands over her face, shuddering in sobs, couldn't answer. She didn't even know why she was crying; it certainly wasn't with pain, but in a sort of desolation. After the intense pleasure she had been through she had come down from a wild peak into this darkness and misery.

Randal pulled her hands down, leaning over to stare at her, then began kissing her wet lids shut, kissing her nose, her cheeks, her trembling lips.

'Stop it, Pippa, stop crying. I'm sorry, don't be unhappy. It was selfish of me, but I was afraid you would vanish again after this weekend, and I couldn't bear it. I had to stop you somehow, make you stay. I thought...'

'Thought what?' she muttered, sat up and grabbed her dress, hurriedly put it on, wishing he wouldn't watch her.

He sighed. 'That if you finally let me make love to you, you'd stay. There's an old legend about a mermaid, who fell in love with a human man, but kept going back into the sea until he made love to her and then she became human and they were married and lived happily.'

'Until one day the call of the sea was too strong and she vanished again, this time for ever,' Pippa recalled.

He grimaced. 'Is that how the legend ends? I only remembered...'

'The bit you wanted to come true?' she mocked. 'How convenient! Well, I'm going to have a shower, and I'd like you to go back to your own room, please.'

'We have to talk!'

'We've done enough talking. Randal, I need to take a shower. Please leave.'

He rolled off the bed and collected up his clothes. She knew she shouldn't watch him, but she couldn't take her eyes off that long, lean, supple, naked body which had just taken her to heaven and back. Randal walked to the door without bothering to dress and she padded barefoot after him to bolt the door behind him.

Wryly, she faced the fact that she was locking the stable door after the horse had bolted. All these years she had avoided making love to him, to anyone, and finally it had happened. She was aching physically, body burning, bruised, weary. What did she do now? She asked herself as she went into the bathroom to shower. What in God's name did she do now?

She discarded her green dress and stepped under the shower, washed from head to foot, the warm water sluicing over her, trying to think, trying to understand how everything had changed over what had just happened.

Randal was right. She groaned, closing her eyes. Oh, he was much too shrewd; he understood her far too well. Nothing would ever be the same again. In taking her just now, he had conquered, had shattered all her arguments, her reasons for saying no to him.

He had realised what she had always known, that she had been dying to make love with him for so long, but had resisted him under the lash of her rational mind—and now it had happened, and she was different. As Randal had intended, she felt differently.

Or did she?

She walked out of the shower and put on a white towelling robe, towelled her damp chestnut hair, looking at herself in the cloudy bathroom mirror. Her green eyes held a bleak realisation now.

Had those moments of bliss and intimacy altered anything? He would still put his son first if it came to it. He would never put her first. She would never matter more to him than anyone else in the world.

Nothing important had changed. She still did not want to accept second place in his life. She still couldn't stay with him; she had to go away.

Like the mermaid in the legend she would have to vanish, this time for ever.

CHAPTER NINE

SHE deliberately chose the most demure outfit she had brought with her: a dove-grey straight skirt, a black chiffon shirt which tied at the waist. Contemplating herself in the mirror, she decided it was exactly the look she wanted for the evening ahead. That last thing she wanted was to look sexy, or put ideas in Randal's head. Her chestnut hair she brushed back and clipped at the nape with a black Spanish comb, leaving her face a clear, cool oval. She wore very little make-up: a faint touch of green on her eyelids, palest pink on her lips. As an afterthought she used a flowery perfume, an English fragrance which drifted about with her, leaving a hint of summer on the air.

She tidied her room, now that all her clothes had been put away, and watched TV for a while, although she found it hard to concentrate.

Randal tapped on her outer door an hour later. She checked on her reflection rapidly before she answered. Yes, that was how she wanted to look—remote, untouchable. As far as possible from the wildly responsive woman he had held in his arms on her bed earlier.

She opened the door and caught a flash of surprise in his eyes. He hadn't expected her to look so serene, and noticed at once the demure way she had dressed.

But he made no comment, simply said, 'If you're ready, I thought we might go downstairs and have tea in the reception area. Renata said she'd bring Johnny back before six, and it's five now.'

'Fine, I'd love a cup of tea,' she said, collecting her handbag, sliding the room key into it. The connecting door was still bolted; it would remain that way as long as they were here. She wanted no repetition of what had happened this afternoon; Randal could stay his side of that door.

Despite her desire to stay cool, though, she felt her pulses leap in that dangerously magnetised fashion when Randal put a hand under her elbow to guide her into the lift. Such a light, polite touch, and yet it sent her body into overdrive.

As the doors shut she hastily moved away from him, and felt his quick, probing glance; he was far too observant, and she did not trust him. But she ignored it. It was better not to say anything, give him any opportunity to gain ground.

Downstairs they sat at a table with a good view of the entrance and ordered a pot of China tea. They drank it without milk, a clear, pale straw-coloured liquid with a delicate fragrance, which was very refreshing.

Out of the corner of her eye she noticed Randal's fingers drumming on the arm of his chair as he watched the entrance. He was agitated over whether or not his ex-wife would bring their son back as promised. She felt a pang of sympathy; poor Randal. He would go crazy if Renata had in fact abducted the child. Would she take the boy abroad, if she did? It could be months before Randal saw Johnny again, in that case, and it would turn his life into a nightmare.

To distract his attention, she said casually, 'I was

thinking, just now, that what I need is a holiday, before I start looking for another job.'

'Where are you thinking of going?'

'Somewhere warm—Spain or Italy, probably. I don't know either country. I've had very few holidays abroad; I could never afford it until I started earning more money at the insurance company, and then I bought my cottage, and that ate up any spare cash I had.'

His grey eyes skimmed her face thoughtfully. 'You've had a pretty tough life, haven't you? No family, no real home, and very little money. It was quite an achievement to buy the cottage and do it up yourself, but at least selling it will release a good lump sum. You'll have money now.'

'Yes, I suppose I will,' she agreed, thinking about it. It would be nice to have spare cash with which she could be spontaneous, which she could spend as she wished, when she wished. She had never been in that position before; every penny she earned had been earmarked for something—clothes, food, travelling expenses to and from work, redecoration on the cottage. 'But then I'll have to buy a new home,' she sighed. 'And it will probably cost far more, so I won't have money for long.'

'If you married me you wouldn't need to buy a new home; you would live in mine,' he said casually, taking her breath away.

'Don't make jokes like that!' She knew he didn't mean it, couldn't mean it, was just teasing her. She looked at him with rage and hostility. 'It isn't funny!'

His grey eyes were serious, though. 'I'm proposing, Pippa. I want to marry you.'

She stared fixedly at her cup of pale tea, fighting

with the stab of jealousy in her stomach. 'You're still
in love with your ex-wife! I realised that at lunch,
when you saw her in the dining room. I saw the look
on your face!'

'I was in shock,' he coolly admitted.

'Oh, yes!' she muttered bitterly. 'I know that. The
sight of her took your breath away.' Renata was stag-
geringly beautiful; she couldn't blame Randal for his
response to the sight of his ex-wife. After all, Renata
had once been his, and now she belonged to another
man. That couldn't be easy to take, especially for a
very ego-driven male like Randal.

She suddenly remembered his jealousy over Tom—
if he felt like that over her, how did he feel over his
ex-wife and her new husband?

'The sight of her scared me!' he said harshly,
frowning. 'I'd stopped expecting her to turn up to see
Johnny. When I saw her I was suddenly worried,
afraid she was going to try to take Johnny away from
me, take him off to Australia. Mothers tend to get
custody in this country, especially if they can afford
a good lawyer, and she can, with her new husband's
money behind her. I thought Renata would never
want custody, she was always an indifferent mother—
but who knows? Maybe her golfer has decided he
wants a ready-made son to trot around the circuits
with him? Good publicity for him, probably.'

She frowned. 'I thought he seemed a decent sort of
guy, not the type to think that way at all.' She looked
at Randal sharply. 'You're simply jealous of him!'

Dark red rang along his cheekbones; his eyes
flashed. 'Don't be absurd! Jealous of him? You're
crazy. Why on earth would I be jealous of him! Over
Renata? I wouldn't have Renata back at any price.'

His grey eyes focused on her angrily. 'I just proposed
to you—doesn't that mean anything to you? All you
do in reply is accuse me of being in love with my ex-
wife! What do you think that tells me? That you don't
know me at all, and, frankly, that I obviously don't
know you either, or how could you leap to such an
idiotic conclusion?'

He was furious with her; she was very shaken, biting her lip. He was right—how could she have leapt
to that conclusion? She didn't know him; she had no
idea what made him tick. How could you love someone without knowing them?

'She is very beautiful,' she offered in apology, in
feeble placation.

His mouth hardened in cynicism. 'On the outside,
maybe, but inside she is far from beautiful. She's selfish, lazy, greedy, materialistic; she was a bad wife
and a bad mother. And I wouldn't have her back for
a million dollars.'

At that second the swing doors into the foyer re-
volved to admit Renata, the tall, tanned golfer, and
Johnny, who saw them immediately and came running towards them.

'Daddy! I played golf! Alex taught me how to play
golf. I hit the ball so hard it went for mile. Alex says
I'm a natural. I should play as often as possible, prac-
tise every day.'

'Don't chatter on and on, darling,' Renata said in
a sort of groan. 'My God, that child babbles. He never
stops.' She sank into a spare chair at the table. 'I need
a drink. Get a waiter, Alex. Randal, darling, I think
Johnny should go to bed; he's tired and so am I—
worn out, honestly. I'd forgotten how much energy
kids have, and how much of a nuisance they are.'

Randal glowered. 'Not in front of him, please!'

'I'll take him upstairs,' Pippa quickly said, getting up. 'Come on, Johnny. I expect you'll need a bath—is he coming down to dinner, Randal?'

'Oh, please,' Johnny said, 'can't I have Room Service and watch TV instead? I'm tired, and I saw they do a great cheeseburger and fries, and a triple flavour ice cream, and Coke.'

Randal laughed. 'Just as you like, Johnny. Room Service would be more fun, I expect. Say goodnight and thank you to your mother and Alex.'

'Goodnight and thank you,' Johnny gabbled towards them, then took Pippa's hand and began dragging her towards the lift.

In the sitting room he at once grabbed the Room Service menu and sat down with it. 'Can I order now? I'm starving.'

'Why not? I'll stay until the food arrives. Do you want me to order it for you?'

He gave her a scornful look. 'I can do it!' Picking up the phone, he began dialling. 'Hello? Room Service?'

Pippa wandered away to the window, listening as he ordered exactly what he had said he would like. The daylight was fading a little, the spring sky coloured pink and gold. Shadows lay under the trees in the grounds of the hotel. It would be dark soon.

Johnny put down the phone. 'They said it would be fifteen minutes.'

She walked back to sit down near him. 'So you had a good time this afternoon.'

'Yes, Alex is great; I like him. My friends all want to meet him. He's a terrific golfer.' He didn't mention his mother, and went on to ask, 'Am I going to be able to ride tomorrow? Dad said I could.'

'Yes, he said he meant to go with you, but I don't have any gear with me, so I think I'll just stay here and rest.'

'Okay,' Johnny said without interest. 'Alex and Mummy are leaving tomorrow, so I don't suppose I'll see them again.' The thought did not seem to bother him. 'She gets bored easily, Alex says. And she doesn't like the country much; she prefers cities. She talked a lot about Sydney and New York and London, and shopping. She loves shopping. Alex says she has so many clothes they had to buy a new wardrobe. She doesn't play golf, although she always goes with Alex when he's playing in a tournament, but she stays in the bar, he said, and waits for him. And she doesn't like kids much; she says she'd never have another one, not ever. Kids are boring.'

'I'm sure she was joking,' Pippa quickly said. How much had that hurt the boy's feelings? Randal was obviously right when he said Renata was a bad mother; how could any mother say such things to her child?

'She wasn't,' Johnny dispassionately said. 'I could tell. She couldn't be bothered. But Alex is okay; I like him.' He found the TV zapper and flicked through the channels. Pippa's heart sank as he settled on a noisy, blaring cartoon.

It was a relief to her when the Room Service waiter knocked on the door and wheeled in a table on which were spread a silver-covered plate of food, a bowl of ice cream nestling in crushed ice, to keep it cool, and several small bottles of cola.

She signed for the food and tipped the waiter, who

left, while Johnny sat up to the table. Pippa tied his napkin round his neck, suspecting its protection for his clothes would be very necessary.

'I'll just go through to my own room,' Pippa said as he picked up his burger and took a bite. 'If you need me, give me a shout.' She didn't think she could stay to watch him eat; melted cheese and tomato ketchup had already spilled out of the burger bun and on to the napkin.

'Uh-huh,' Johnny said, turning up the TV and feeding chips into his chewing mouth.

Pippa left the connecting door open in case Johnny needed her, then settled down on her bed with a book she had brought with her: a paperback detective story by one of her favourite authors. It wasn't easy to concentrate on the pages, though, with the boom of Johnny's TV in her ears.

After a while she went back to see how he was doing and found him sprawled on the floor on his tummy. Pippa rearranged the table and wheeled it out of the suite, left it in the corridor, then rang Room Service to ask them to collect it.

'Why don't you get into your pyjamas now and watch TV in bed?' she suggested to Johnny, who enthusiastically agreed. 'Better wash and clean your teeth first,' Pippa casually added, an idea to which he was less enthusiastic.

'You don't want your daddy to see you with tomato ketchup all over your face, do you?' she gently said, and he grimaced horribly.

'Oh, okay, then.' He went into the bathroom and was back a minute later. 'Can I have a shower?'

'Of course.'

He was in the bathroom for twenty minutes. Pippa

wondered a little anxiously what he was doing in there, and hoped he wouldn't leave the room looking as if a bomb had gone off, but eventually he emerged looking very clean in his pyjamas and climbed into one of the twin beds, clutching the TV remote control.

Pippa turned off the main light but left his bedside lamp lit. 'I'll be in the next room if you want me,' she said, leaving him. 'Goodnight, Johnny.'

'Goodnight, Pip,' he said, then gave her a grin. 'Do you mind if I call you Pip?'

'All my life people have called me Pip.' She smiled, not adding that she hated the name.

Going through into her own bedroom she changed rapidly into the cocktail dress she had brought with her; a delicate fantasy of different shades of green silk and chiffon, falling to her mid-calf in a flurry, with a scooped neckline and tiny frilled sleeves. She found a silver chain in her bag, from which hung a dark green stone and a silver tassel. Around her throat it gave exactly the right touch to the outfit.

She knew she would never hold a candle to Renata's blonde magnificence, but at least she looked her best, she decided.

A quarter of an hour later, Randal let himself into the suite and found Pippa reading, curled up on the sitting room couch. She lifted her head to survey him expressionlessly, and he in turn contemplated her with what she saw with a gulp of shock to be rage. His grey eyes were molten steel, his mouth taut.

Breathing thickly, he finally erupted, 'What the hell do you think you are doing up here? We were supposed to be having dinner with Renata and Alex; we've been waiting for you for half an hour.'

'Sorry, I was taking care of Johnny and I forgot

the time,' she apologised anxiously. He looked so angry it made her mouth dry and her heart beat harder.

'Where is Johnny?'

'In bed, watching TV.'

He turned on his heel and stalked through into his own bedroom. The burble of the TV stopped, the faint gleam of light was switched off, then he came back.

'He's asleep.'

'Oh, good, I expect he was very tired after all the excitement of today,' she said, getting up and collecting her handbag. 'But we had better leave a low light on in here, and the door open so he can see it, in case he wakes up alone in the dark and gets scared. I explained to him that he could ring Reception and ask for us to be paged, if he needs us.'

'Good idea,' approved Randal. 'Did he eat?'

'Burger, chips and ice cream—yes, quite a lot. And he had a shower. After he was in bed I thought I'd better stay within earshot, in case he needed me.'

'You're very thoughtful.'

'I remember how scared I was of the dark when I was nine.' She shrugged dismissively. But there had been nobody to come to her rescue, then; her foster parents had dismissed her fear of the dark as childish, and told her to pull herself together.

Randal took her arm and hurried her towards the door. 'It was me who needed you, downstairs, helping me to put up with Renata.'

He did not say thank you, she noted—no Thank you for looking after my little boy; no Thank you for going to so much trouble on my behalf! All he was doing was complaining because she hadn't been downstairs with him to protect him from his ex-wife. Men were incredibly selfish creatures.

'I couldn't be in two places at once!'

He urged her into the lift, which started with a jerk which sent her sprawling sideways into him, grabbing at him to stop herself falling on the floor.

His arm came round her, supporting her, holding her close to him, and she felt her treacherous body shudder with awareness.

His head shifted so that he could look down into her wide, disturbed green eyes. She looked away, unable to meet that stare, afraid of what her eyes must be revealing. She must not give away too much; she had already betrayed too much to him. She wanted to clamp a mask on her face from now on, stop him guessing any more about her.

'Pippa, don't look like that,' he murmured huskily, and his mouth came down, skimmed hers for a second before the lift stopped, and he straightened before guiding her out of the lift.

His arm was round her waist, his hand beneath her breast; she was afraid he could feel the fierce beating of her heart, the raggedness of her breathing. Every time he touched her, looked at her, there was this wild reaction; she couldn't stop it. The sooner she could get away from him the sooner she might start to feel safe. At the moment she was living moment to moment, like someone on the very edge of a live volcano.

'You look lovely,' he suddenly told her. 'I love that dress, all those shades of green. And your hair looks wonderful against them, a perfect match, chestnut and green. You look like spring itself.'

She flushed, her throat trembling in pleasure. 'Thank you.'

'Renata and Alex have gone into the dining room;

they'll be waiting at the table,' he told her as they walked through the foyer.

'Has Renata changed for dinner, too?'

'Yes, she put on something black, very formal. I've always been turned off by the sight of women in black; it makes me feel I'm going to a funeral.'

When Pippa saw Renata a moment later she had to be incredulous about Randal's comment. The 'something black' he had said Renata was wearing was body-hugging, sleek, daring black satin with a plunging neckline, revealing a great deal of golden skin and the deep valley between her high breasts, curving down into her small waist and swelling out again, smoothly, over her hips, ending at her knees.

She looked sensational; men at every other table were staring, hardly conscious of what they were eating, while the other women in the room looked daggers at her. There was nothing funereal about her whatever.

'Is that what you call formal?' Pippa whispered to Randal as they walked towards the table.

'Black always is, isn't it?'

'Not when it looks like that!'

A trio was playing light, popular music, seated on a dais in a corner of the room—a pianist, a drummer, a trombone player. Diners talked over them; the room was quite crowded and bustling with waiters coming and going.

As they joined the other two Alex rose, smiling. 'Hello, Pippa, you look very pretty. What an unusual dress.'

'Thank you,' she said, then turned to smile at Renata. 'And you are causing a sensation in that dress, as if you didn't know!'

Renata sipped a champagne cocktail, purring like a cat that had swallowed cream. 'Why, thanks, that's sweet of you. Now, read the menu and choose your meal; I'm ravenous! I ate a small lunch, now I need something more substantial.'

Pippa glanced quickly at the menu, which was rather more extensive than the lunchtime menu, decided on minestrone soup followed by chicken Stroganoff with rice.

The waiter came along to take their order. As he left again, Alex asked her, 'Did Johnny get Room Service?'

'Yes, cheeseburger and fries!'

'I wouldn't mind that, myself. I guess I'm primitive—I prefer junk food to the sort of posh stuff they serve here. Mind you, I have to eat a lot of salads and fruit, to keep my weight down. You can't have a fat golfer, not if you want to win tournaments. Is Johnny okay up there on his own, do you think?'

'He was asleep when we left him, but I told him to ring Reception if he woke up and felt frightened.' She glanced at Renata, who was toying with her champagne flute, looking bored. 'I'm sorry I kept you waiting; I was making sure Johnny settled down in bed.'

Alex gave her a warm, reassuring smile. 'That's okay, it was kind of you to take care of him. He's a good kid. I've got quite fond of him. I promised to take him to one of my tournaments some time. He seemed keen to come along. His friends at school are golf fans, he told me; some of them play at a course near the school. I think he wants to impress them.' He looked at Randal. 'If that's okay with you?'

'In principle, yes, but remember, he's at school a

lot of the time and can't just go off for the day. In the summer holidays he has plenty of free time, but not at other times of the year.'

'Oh, don't worry, Randal, we don't want to drag around with the kid in tow too often, whining and wanting burgers all the time,' Renata said with a snap. 'He's a nuisance, always wanting attention. Unless we hire a nanny to take care of him. I guess we could do that. I can't wait for him to grow up a little. I wouldn't mind a teenager hanging around, someone you can talk to. But little kids are a pain.'

'You're his mother, for God's sake! You're supposed to love him, enjoy taking care of him!' erupted Randal, glaring at her. 'Pippa has ten times more patience with him than you do!'

Renata gave Pippa a derisive glance. 'Yes, well, Pippa's obviously the maternal type, doesn't mind running around after a spoilt, whiny kid.'

Dark red colour splashed Randal's cheeks. 'Johnny is not spoilt, nor is he whiny!'

Alex chimed in, 'No, he isn't. He's fun, a great kid!' He made an apologetic gesture. 'But Renata simply isn't the motherly type, you know.'

'No, I'm certainly not!' she said, tossing her head, the diamond earrings dangling from her ears swinging to and fro.

Alex added, 'Some women are, some aren't.'

'We're not all the same!' Renata drawled, giving Pippa another of those dismissive looks.

Alex said, 'Maybe Pippa has the sort of mother who's a maternal role model, the type who loves kids, cooks, cleans the house—all those old-fashioned things a modern woman doesn't want to waste her life doing.'

'Is it a waste of life?' queried Pippa. 'You think so?' Her tone made it clear she didn't agree.

'Well, no, I guess not, if that's what you enjoy,' Alex placated, smiling at her. 'But Renata's mother was a career woman who left her with a nanny and never bothered about her—you can understand why Renata isn't the motherly type when you know that.'

Brusquely, Randal retorted, 'Pippa is an orphan. She had no mother at all, and grew up in orphanages and foster homes. She had no motherly role model.'

It made her feel odd to hear him defending her, explaining her. She was touched; maybe he understood her better than she had imagined.

Alex looked at her with sympathy. 'That must have been tough; not a fun childhood, I guess. I bet you're dying to have a family now, to finally have all the things you never had as a child.'

'Yes, I suppose so,' Pippa admitted, feeling Randal's eyes on her profile.

Renata drawled. 'Which explains why you're so keen to take care of Johnny! You get a ready-made family right off.'

Their first course arrived in time to save Pippa answering that; she felt resentment burning in her throat and would have liked to slap Renata's face. Instead, she concentrated on the food. When conversation did start again it was Randal, asking Alex about his golf success, and Pippa didn't have to join in; she just sat there, listening. Every so often Renata leaned towards Randal and spoke softly to him, sometimes letting her red-tipped fingernails drift along his sleeve, smiling at him, her long, false lashes flicking up and down.

He watched her with an expression in his eyes that Pippa could not read. At times she felt he disliked his ex-wife; at other times she thought he was still fascinated by her, sexually responsive to her.

Renata was so beautiful. How could any man not be responsive to looks like that? She radiated sex appeal.

'Do you like sport, Pippa?' Alex asked her, and the other two turned to stare at her.

'I like watching it; Wimbledon, for instance. I always enjoy that on TV. But I wouldn't say I was the sporting type. I've never had the time; I've always had to work too hard. I'm afraid I've never even played golf, or watched it. And it's an expensive sport, isn't it? You need clubs and the right shoes, and stuff.'

'Johnny said something about going riding this weekend,' Renata said. 'Are you two going with him?'

'I shall, but Pippa probably won't,' Randal told her.

'I haven't got the right gear,' she said, meeting Renata's contemptuous smile with dislike.

When they were drinking their coffee after the meal people began dancing on a small parquet floor in front of the band's dais. Renata stood up, held out her hand to Randal.

'Shall we?'

He hesitated, but eventually rose and took her hand. They threaded their way through the tables and began to dance the waltz being played. Jealousy stung inside Pippa; she looked down, reluctant to watch them, Randal's arm around his ex-wife's waist, her arm around his neck, their bodies very close, moving in harmony.

'Would you care to dance, Pippa?' Alex asked her

without real enthusiasm, and she shook her head, smiling politely.

'Sorry, I'm too tired.'

'It's not a very good band,' he grimaced.

She laughed. 'No.'

A moment later a waiter came over to them and bent to murmur in her ear, 'Reception has had a message from your suite, madam. Your little boy seems to be upset.'

She was on her feet immediately, relieved to have an excuse for leaving. 'Thank you, I'll go up to him.' She smiled at Alex. 'Please give my excuses to Renata and Randal. It was a pleasure to meet you. Goodnight.'

When she got upstairs and let herself into the suite she heard low sobbing from the double bedroom and hurried through there at once. Johnny was a heap in the bed, lying on his face, crying quietly. Pippa sat down on the bed and lifted him, turning him towards her.

'What's wrong?'

He hiccuped. 'I had a nightmare.'

His face was damp and flushed, his eyes wet. Pippa laid him down again and went to the bathroom, ran water over a flannel, squeezed some of the water out before taking it to bathe Johnny's hot face.

She got him orange juice from the mini fridge in the room, brushed his tangled hair back from his face, made him sit up to drink his juice.

'What was the nightmare about?'

'I was being chased by something. I couldn't see what it was, it was dark, but it made horrid noises.'

'I hate dreams like that,' she said, and his small body fitted itself against her heavily.

'Do you have them?'

'Oh, yes, everyone does, even grown-ups—they're the worst, because you don't know what's after you.'

He finished his juice. She took the glass from him as he yawned.

'Tired?' she murmured, helping him to lie down again. 'You go back to sleep; I'll stay here. You only have to yell and I'll come running.'

His eyes had closed; in the lamplight she saw his lashes flutter down against his flushed cheeks. What had he been dreaming about? she wondered. What monsters haunted his sleep?

When she was sure he was breathing rhythmically, fast asleep, she tiptoed out into the sitting room, leaving one lamp burning beside the bed, in case Johnny woke again.

Going into her own bathroom, she undressed, washed, put on a white silk nightdress and matching robe, brushed her chestnut hair, then returned to the sitting room and lay down on the couch to read her book. She did not want to be out of earshot in case Johnny called her.

At some point she fell asleep; the book slipped to the floor. She did not have nightmares; she was too tired to dream.

She woke with a start, hearing a sound, and looked up to find Randal sitting beside her, his fingers stroking her cheek.

'Oh, hello,' she said, startled, shifting to dislodge his hand. 'Did Alex explain why I left? Johnny had a nightmare, but he's asleep again now.'

'I know. I checked just now. He's deeply asleep. Thanks for coming up to take care of him.'

'That's okay.' Under his possessive stare she was

suddenly conscious of her bare legs, of her semi-transparent nightdress, the silk clinging to her warm body, her breasts visible at the low neckline. 'Well, I'll go to bed myself now and leave you to take care of Johnny.' She tried to slide off the couch but Randal was in the way, his lean body blocking her escape route.

As he bent his head she wailed, 'No, Randal!'

It was a vain protest. His mouth hit hers with a demand that left her too weak to fight the seductive sensuality of that kiss, the caressing hands roaming over her, stroking her bare throat, her shoulders, sliding down inside the nightdress to touch her breasts, wandering up over her bare legs, while all the time she quivered, drawn by the magnetic power of Randal's body against hers.

She knew what would happen if she didn't stop him, yet she was helpless to do a thing about his lovemaking. Every inch of her was shuddering with pleasure under his hands, his mouth; she ached to have him inside her again, to be taken to that wild peak of ecstasy.

Then they both heard a stir in the further room, a whimper from the child sleeping in there, and Randal sat up, his head turned that way, listening.

Pippa took her opportunity and wriggled out from the couch. 'You'd better go and see if he's okay,' she said, and fled, trembling, before Randal could stop her.

CHAPTER TEN

NEXT morning, as they ate a very late breakfast downstairs, Renata and Alex came in to say goodbye. Alex was casual in jeans and a bright yellow sweatshirt. Renata was dressed as for some grand occasion, a film premiére, perhaps, or a fashionable cocktail party, wearing a skintight sky-blue dress with hardly any back and very little above the waist at the front. Other guests, eating egg and bacon or fresh fruit, stopped to goggle in disbelief at this vision.

Her son looked pinkly embarrassed; his mother was not dressed the way he thought mothers should dress at breakfast time.

Randal's brows rose but he was very polite.

'Have a safe trip, and let us know in advance next time you're coming to see Johnny.' He held out a hand. 'Nice to talk to you, Alex; I must bring Johnny along to watch you play some time soon.'

'I'd like that,' Alex said, shaking hands.

'Me, too,' Johnny eagerly chimed in, and everyone smiled indulgently at the boy.

Alex shook hands with Pippa, who was dressed in a pleated brown skirt and dark green sweater, very differently from Renata. 'I enjoyed getting to know you, Pippa. I hope we'll meet again.'

She smiled back. 'Nice to meet you, Alex.'

Renata looked pointedly at her watch. 'We ought to be getting on our way. Do come along, Alex!' She didn't bother with courtesies; she wanted to get away as soon as possible, and made that clear.

Alex obeyed, his expression a little wry. People watched them leave, whispering—no doubt many of them recognised Alex, who was, after all, quite famous.

Renata hadn't spoken to, let alone kissed her son, Pippa realised, wondering if the boy had been hurt. She found Renata's indifference to the pain she might inflict baffling. What sort of woman was she? Across the table her eyes met Randal's; he grimaced silently at her. He had noticed that Renata had ignored their son, too. There wasn't much Randal ever missed.

He returned his attention to the fresh fruit and croissants he was eating. Johnny had decided on a full English breakfast, which he claimed he ate at school most mornings. Pippa couldn't even look at his food; it made her feel sick. She was eating fresh figs and Greek yoghurt, then she might eat a slice of toast.

'This morning, I thought we'd go for a walk around the hotel grounds,' Randal suggested. 'Unless you want to do some shopping, Pippa. There's a large discount shopping centre a few miles away—would you like to go there?'

She shook her head. 'I'd rather go for a walk.'

Johnny beamed at her. 'There's a crazy golf course here; we could have a game.'

'Why not? I've never played any sort of golf, but I don't mind trying my hand.'

'You'll soon learn,' Johnny paternally assured her. 'I'll teach you. I'm quite good, for my age—Alex said so.'

The weather was bright but a little blustery and

slightly cool. The walk was very enjoyable and the game of crazy golf had her and Johnny in fits of laughter. Randal played, too, but seemed abstracted.

Johnny won the game and Pippa bought him an ice cream back at the hotel, as a prize. He took it upstairs to the suite with him and ate it watching the inevitable cartoons on the TV in the bedroom.

Pippa and Randal retreated to the sitting room. She curled up in an armchair; he sat down on the couch close by.

'I talked to the riding stables. They do have some boots and hats for hire,' Randal said. 'But no jodhpurs. They said you could wear jeans, though. You've got some with you, haven't you?'

'Yes, but I'd rather not ride, if you don't mind. I think it would be good for you to be alone with Johnny, for one thing. For another, I'm not wild about riding horses. And I thought I'd take a siesta this afternoon. I've had a very tiring week, one way and another; I need a long rest.'

He nodded soberly. 'Yes, no doubt it's been traumatic, but at least it's all over now, and you know the outcome has been good for you. You'd have been insane to marry Tom; he's a decent enough guy but he's as dull as ditchwater and you didn't love him.'

'Don't talk about him!' she muttered, keeping a wary eye on the door in case Johnny appeared there. 'You don't know what you're talking about!'

'I know you love me,' he coolly informed her, taking her breath away.

She sat upright, face flushing dark red, then turning white. 'You know nothing of the kind! Your vanity is mind-blowing. What on earth makes you think I love you? I've got more sense.'

He sat down on the arm of her chair, caught her face between his palms and kissed her fiercely. She couldn't escape or avoid that devouring mouth, and after a moment of writhing indignation she stopped wanting to, her lips quivering under his, her arms going round his neck.

Without lifting his mouth, he whispered, 'Tell me, Pippa. Tell me you love me. Stop lying to me, and yourself. I love you; you know that. Yesterday I discovered you love me too; you'd never given yourself to me if you didn't. So, tell me! I need to hear you saying it.'

A single tear rolled down from under her closed lids. She gave a small, pathetic sob, pushing at his powerful chest, trying to make him let go of her.

'All you ever think about is what you need. What about what I need?'

'What's that?'

'Time,' she groaned. 'Time to think. I'm so confused. A week ago I was planning my marriage to Tom. Now here I am, with you. I feel as if I've been through an earthquake. The landscape of my life has been torn up; I don't know where I am, or what I want to do. And you keep pushing me, trying to make me do what you want me to do! Leave me alone, Randal. Give me some time and space to work out how I really feel!'

He studied her, frowning, then dropped a light kiss on her nose. 'Okay, we'll talk about it some other time. But you do like Johnny, don't you? I've been watching you with him; I can see you do. I know you said you wanted to be first with anyone you married, not come second after their child—but that was before you got to know Johnny. Do you still feel the same?'

She worried her lower lip, sighing. 'I don't know. No, I suppose not. Seeing him with his mother, I felt so sorry for him. I had a loveless childhood, myself—that's why I badly want to be loved, to come first with the man I marry. I can understand where Johnny's coming from, though; I've been through what he's going through. And I think it's worse for him, because he does have a mother who's alive, but seems quite indifferent to him, whereas I had nobody. I was lonely and neglected but I wasn't getting hurt the way Johnny is.'

Grimly, Randal said, 'Renata's a selfish woman who puts herself first, always has. You see, that's what happens when a woman demands to come first.'

'That's not fair!' she protested angrily. 'I never said I'd put myself first if I ever had a child!'

'No, I believe you wouldn't, but Renata does, always has. There's no room in her life for a child. The less Johnny sees of her, the better. He won't get so badly hurt if he doesn't see her too often. But I don't want him blaming me, telling himself I kept her away. I have to let her visit him if she ever feels like it, although I wish I could stop her seeing him.'

They kept their voices very low, neither of them wanting the boy to hear what they were saying.

'I made a terrible mistake when I married her,' Randal dryly said. 'If I'd known what she was really like I wouldn't have got involved, but I was a lot younger, and she was really lovely.

'Still is.' Pippa shrugged. 'Don't deny you couldn't stop looking at her; I saw you staring.'

His mouth quirked sideways in amusement. 'Well, she is quite a knock-out! In fact, I'd say she's lovelier now than ever. She knows how to dress and use make-up.' He gave her a mocking smile. 'I knew you were jealous, little green eyes!'

'I was not!' she flared immediately, and he laughed.

'Oh, yes, you were. But you didn't need to be! I told you that yesterday. Yes, she's drop-dead gorgeous, but I'm not a romantic boy any more. I want a woman to have a lot of other qualities. Beauty isn't everything. In fact, beauty isn't very much at all. It's just a façade. To be a real woman you need a heart, warmth, caring. And I want a woman with a sense of humour, brains...all Renata offers is what she looks like, and that isn't enough for me now.'

His grey eyes were deadly serious; she had doubted him yesterday but now she was ready to believe him. She had seen the cynicism in his face as he watched his ex-wife. Renata didn't take him in.

Johnny ran into the room a moment later and his father got up to greet him, raking back his slightly dishevelled black hair.

'Hello, enjoyed your cartoons?'

'Yeah. When are we having lunch?' the boy demanded.

Randal looked at his watch, made a surprised face. 'It's half past twelve. Do you want to go down now?'

'Yes, please.'

'You've got ice cream round your mouth,' Pippa gently reminded him. 'Maybe we should all go to the bathroom before we leave?'

'Okay.' Johnny streaked away and his father shuddered.

'I wish I had his energy! Not to mention his stomach. He's hardly digested that ice cream but already he's thinking about more food!'

'He's a growing boy!' Pippa grinned; she found Johnny's unashamed delight in food amusing. But then she liked the boy a lot; in some ways he reminded her of his father, in other ways he was very much himself. She had grown very fond of him.

After lunch Johnny and Randal changed into their riding clothes to go to the stables. Pippa curled up on a couch in the sitting room and watched a TV programme.

While Johnny was putting on his boots, Randal said quietly to her, 'You're sure you won't come?'

She shook her head, keeping her face blank. 'I'd rather stay here and rest.'

He hesitated, eyeing her shrewdly. 'I hope you aren't planning to bolt again? You will be here when we get back?'

She tossed her hair back, making a face. 'Oh, don't be tiresome! Just go, will you?'

Johnny appeared before Randal had the chance to say anything else, and the two of them left.

As soon as they had gone Pippa hurried into her bedroom and packed everything. She could not stay here; she had a sense of impending disaster. It was blindingly obvious that if she didn't get away she would find herself being stampeded into marrying Randal, and every time she thought about that violent alarm bells went off inside her head and heart.

She took her case down to Reception and asked them to get her a taxi to the nearest railway station.

'Will the other members of your party be staying on, or are they leaving too?' the receptionist asked, looking at her suspiciously, obviously wondering if she was bolting without paying the bill.

'Yes, they're staying tonight, but they've gone riding at the local stables. They should be back in a couple of hours. Their luggage is all upstairs.'

The receptionist rang a taxi firm, then told her, 'The cab should be here in ten minutes.'

She sat down and waited, gazing out into the hotel grounds. The trees tossed restlessly in the brisk wind but the sun was shining and wallflowers in a large raised bed sent waves of strong scent into the hotel foyer.

The taxi arrived and drove her to the railway station. She was lucky; there was a train to London only a quarter of an hour later. She got to town in time to catch her connecting train into Essex and was back at her cottage by six.

Her nerves were on edge, wondering if Randal would ring, but the evening passed without hearing from him.

She made herself scrambled egg on toast for supper and went to bed quite early, feeling absolutely exhausted. She woke up in the night crying, tears pouring down her face after a dream she couldn't remember at all except that it had left her with a sense of terrible loss and loneliness.

She got up and went downstairs, made herself hot chocolate and took it back to bed, sat up against banked pillows sipping it, trying to remember what her dream had been about. She couldn't track it down, though, just remember the feelings.

The trouble was, her mind was in confusion: torn, divided, constantly swinging between dread of seeing Randal again, of having to face his insistence that she must marry him, and a yearning to be with him, to be in his arms, in his bed.

He was right, of course; now that she had got to

know Johnny she liked him, was already fond of him. Randal had shrewdly guessed that that would happen. By introducing her to his son he had hoped to disarm her and he had done it. She knew she no longer resented Johnny's place in his father's affections, no longer wanted Randal to put her first at his son's expense. How could she want to supplant that poor, sad little boy, whose mother couldn't be bothered with him, who had been starved of Renata's affection all his short life?

Johnny was a lively, intelligent child who mostly hid his emotional problems, but Pippa had learnt that they existed, had seen the boy's hurt response to his mother's rejection.

No, she no longer wanted to come first with Randal. Johnny needed his father's love as much as she did.

But she still couldn't marry Randal. She had been puzzled at first, hadn't been able to work out why she was so scared, but in the silence of that spring night she faced up to the reasons. She couldn't take the risk. It was that simple. She was scared. Marrying Randal would be like bungee jumping off a cliff, afraid the rope would break, afraid she would hit the ground and be killed or horribly maimed.

She had been emotionally maimed last time. Four years ago she had had the guts to walk away from him, but she had been damaged by doing it. When they'd met again she had rationalised her instinctive need for flight, for getting away from him, had told herself it was because he had chosen his wife and child over her before and she needed a man who would put her first every time, but now she knew it hadn't been that at all.

She was simply afraid of getting hurt again. It was a case of the burnt child fearing the fire. She couldn't take the risk.

Finishing her hot chocolate, she switched off the lamp and lay down in the dark. She must clear her mind of Randal, mustn't let herself think about him, must not keep turning over thoughts of him. She had to get some sleep. She was so tired. And no more dreams!

The answer was to think of something else. A holiday! That would keep her mind busy. Where should she go? Spain? Italy? At this time of year anywhere in the Mediterranean would be wonderful—not too hot, not too crowded. She must go to a travel agent and book herself two weeks in some lovely place.

She would probably go to a seaside resort, but one which could offer fascinating places to visit too. Somehow Italy seemed to her at this moment to offer more. She would get a brochure and choose somewhere. Anywhere, it didn't matter where, because she knew nothing much about Italy. Wherever she went it would be new and exciting.

She must have fallen asleep quite quickly because the next time she woke up it was morning and the room was full of golden light.

It was a lovely morning; spring was slowly turning into summer, the lilacs were out in clusters of white and purple, the roses were budding and the air was rich with the scent of blossom.

Pippa got up, showered, put on jeans and a white T-shirt, blow-dried her chestnut hair, then went downstairs for breakfast.

She had bran cereal with fresh fruit, which she sliced into her bowl: apple, banana, grapes. With it she drank a small glass of orange juice and then a cup of black coffee. After that she did some housework and then went out into the garden to mow the lawn.

While she was doing that Tom arrived, came round the side of the house to find her.

'Where have you been?' he demanded.

Switching off the mower, she smiled at him, pushing back her hair from her sun-flushed face.

'Hello, Tom. I was visiting a friend.'

'What friend?' He had that belligerent look she was coming to recognise. 'I suppose you mean Harding?'

'Tom, don't start on one of those inquisitions. I don't have to tell you who I see, or where I go. So don't bark at me.'

He made a growling noise in his throat like an angry dog and showed his teeth. 'We may not be getting married, but I still worry about you. The man's pure poison. Stay away from him!'

'I'm not discussing him with you, any more than I'd discuss you with him!'

'What does he say about me?' he broke out, very red in the face.

She groaned. 'Oh, for heaven's sake, Tom! Why are you here and what do you want?'

After a seething pause, he said, 'I wanted to work out a timetable for the sale of the house. I can put down a deposit whenever you like, but when, exactly, do you want to exchange contracts?'

She took off her gardening gloves. 'Come in and have a coffee and we'll work something out.'

They sat in the kitchen, drinking coffee and writing out a proposed timetable for the sale.

'I don't want you to feel you're being forced out,'

Tom assured her. 'You suggest a date when it would be convenient for you to move out, then if you need to stay on for a while we can adjust the date later.'

'You're very thoughtful, Tom,' she said, smiling at him. He was a kind man, too; she appreciated the way he tried to make things easier for her. If only he would stop trying to interfere in her life!

'Have you decided where to go on holiday?' he asked.

She shook her head. 'I'll check that out tomorrow. What about you? I thought you would be going away today; that was the plan originally, wasn't it?'

'I had to change the flights. I rang to explain that I'd only need one seat, so they suggested I went tomorrow. It's easier to sell two seats than one, they said. More couples go on these holiday flights. So I'm off early tomorrow. That's why I had to see you today, before I went.'

'Well, I hope you have a lovely time, Tom.'

'I intend to!' He looked at his watch. 'Look, come and have lunch at the pub—you've always liked their roast Sunday lunch.'

It seemed a good idea, it would save her having to cook a meal for herself, so she agreed and they left ten minutes later. The pub was only half full when they arrived, but as time wore on more and more people crowded into the timbered room, with its shining horse brasses and silver tankards hanging on the wall behind the bar counter.

They both chose carrot soup followed by roast beef with light, crispy Yorkshire pudding, roast potatoes, carrots and Brussels sprouts.

'Their gravy's terrific, too,' Tom said, as he finished. 'Not to mention the horseradish sauce.'

They knew a few of the other customers and got into a game of billiards after the meal. It was nearly four o'clock before Tom drove Pippa home.

'Thank you for lunch; it was great,' she said. 'Do you want to come in for tea or coffee?'

'I have to pack, yet,' he said. 'I'd better scoot home now.'

'Have a wonderful holiday!' she said, and stood waving as he drove away.

She was grateful to him for having taken up the whole afternoon. If Randal had pursued her here he would have found her not at home, so she would have avoided a difficult confrontation.

If only she could fix a holiday at once! Then she would be able to put off seeing Randal for weeks. For the rest of the day she was on tenterhooks, and was very relieved when night fell and she could lock up the cottage and go to bed to read and listen to music.

There were no bad dreams that night and she slept well. When she got up it was raining, a light, thin rain which came in sudden showers. She showered, dressed, had breakfast, then did some housework.

Mid-morning, she drove to the nearest travel agent, was given a brochure of Italian holidays and took it across the road to a café, where she read it, drinking another cup of coffee.

Tom would be in the air by now, *en route* for what would have been their honeymoon. Lucky Tom.

She was attracted by the idea of a fortnight on the Adriatic coast; there she could combine a beach holiday with a visit to the Byzantine church at Ravenna and a trip to Venice, which she had always longed to see. So she went back to the travel agent and booked two weeks at a hotel right on the beach road, with full board, starting in a week's time. She would fly there, of course, from Gatwick Airport, and would be taken by coach to her hotel.

A trouble-free holiday, she decided. She couldn't wait.

After doing some shopping she drove home to find Randal's car parked outside the cottage, with him sitting in the driving seat.

While he watched her sardonically, she sat in her own car, paralysed, drumming her fingers restlessly on the wheel, feeling like driving off again and staying out until she could be sure he would have gone. But what was the point? She could put it off, but sooner or later Randal would catch up with her; she knew how persistent he could be.

So she drove on to her forecourt and parked. As she got out of her car, Randal got out of his, but she ignored him, hurrying to open her front door. Before she could shut it in his face he was beside her, pushing his way inside on her heels.

'Where have you been?' he demanded, as Tom had done yesterday.

'Shopping and booking a Mediterranean holiday,' she defiantly told him, walking into the kitchen with her shopping basket and beginning to unpack what she had bought.

'You'll have to cancel that,' he said with calm arrogance. 'We'll go abroad for our honeymoon!'

'There isn't going to be one!' she snapped.

He coolly put the kettle on and got out the instant coffee, just as if he lived here too, set out two mugs, got milk from the fridge, then leaned against the kitchen counter, watching her.

'Make yourself at home,' she said with irritation. Who did he think he was?

'I've just been to Tom's place,' he drawled. 'But there was no sign of him. His next door neighbour told me he was away, on his honeymoon!'

She finished unpacking and put her shopping basket away, not commenting. Randal's grey eyes had a dangerous glitter.

'I thought maybe you'd changed your mind and married him after all!'

'No,' she calmly answered, and his eyes flashed like lightning.

Moving with pantherish grace and speed, he caught hold of her, pushed her up against the wall, holding her there with his own body, forcing her to confront him.

'Don't try to be funny!'

'I wasn't. You asked if I'd married Tom, I said no; that's all!'

'I was out of my mind,' Randal grated. Inches away, his face was white with rage. 'I couldn't be sure you wouldn't do anything so stupid! I just don't understand you. But I was terrified you might have done it just to get away from me.'

Her heart crashed like a burning plane. She couldn't breathe properly, couldn't meet his probing, furious eyes.

'You promised me you'd be at the hotel when Johnny and I got back from the riding stables,' he accused. 'But the minute we'd left you packed and went. They told me at Reception. Why? Why did you run away again? You said you liked Johnny, and I know you want me...'

'No,' she denied. 'That's the point. I don't.'

'Liar.' He caught her face between his hands and kissed her hotly, sensuously, making her legs give way under her. 'Do I have to show you all over again? I'll make love to you in here, on the floor, if I have to. You want me. Admit it.'

'That's just sex,' she huskily conceded.

'Call it what you like. You want me. I can have you any time I feel like it.'

'How dare you?' she angrily broke out. 'I'm not some bimbo you can just...' She stopped, so insulted she couldn't get another word out.

'I didn't say you were! You may call it sex, but we both know it's love. That's what we feel for each other. So why do you keep running away?'

She closed her eyes, a sob forming in her throat, salty tears welling behind her lids.

'I can't take the risk!'

'What risk?' he impatiently insisted.

'Of getting hurt. Last time I nearly died of misery; it was months before I got over losing you. Now I'm afraid of...oh, of everything. How I feel, what might happen if I do marry you, getting hurt again if it doesn't work out between us, the future—everything!'

He put his warm mouth on her wet eyes, kissed them gently, slid his mouth down her cheeks, whispering between kisses, 'I didn't realise you were such a coward. Pippa, darling, I love you and I want to be with you for ever. Do you want to be with me? And don't lie this time. Tell the truth. Do you want to be with me for the rest of our lives?'

She made a wailing noise, keeping her eyes shut. 'Don't ask...'

His mouth touched hers gently. 'I am asking. Tell

me the truth. Do you love me? Do you want to be with me for ever?'

She drew breath, shuddering, then took the final terrifying leap into the truth. 'Yes. Yes.'

He drew her even closer, held her, his mouth against her hair, rocking her as if she was a baby.

'I love you. Say it too.'

'Yes,' she groaned. 'I love you. I love you.'

And felt the fear and tension draining out of her body. She had been afraid of love all this time, afraid of giving herself, of getting hurt, afraid of life itself.

Now she wasn't; she never would be again. She wound her arms around his neck and gave herself up to him, kissing him passionately, with unleashed desire.

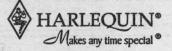

CALL THE ONES YOU LOVE OVER THE HOLIDAYS!

Save $25 off future book purchases when you buy any four Harlequin® or Silhouette® books in October, November and December 2001,

PLUS

receive a phone card good for 15 minutes of long-distance calls to anyone you want in North America!

WHAT AN INCREDIBLE DEAL!

Just fill out this form and attach 4 proofs of purchase (cash register receipts) from October, November and December 2001 books, and Harlequin Books will send you a coupon booklet worth a total savings of $25 off future purchases of Harlequin® and Silhouette® books, AND a 15-minute phone card to call the ones you love, anywhere in North America.

Please send this form, along with your cash register receipts as proofs of purchase, to:
In the USA: Harlequin Books, P.O. Box 9057, Buffalo, NY 14269-9057
In Canada: Harlequin Books, P.O. Box 622, Fort Erie, Ontario L2A 5X3
Cash register receipts must be dated no later than December 31, 2001.
Limit of 1 coupon booklet and phone card per household.
Please allow 4-6 weeks for delivery.

I accept your offer! Enclosed are 4 proofs of purchase. Please send me my coupon booklet and a 15-minute phone card:

Name: _____

Address: _____ City: _____

State/Prov.: _____ Zip/Postal Code: _____

Account Number (if available): _____

---

097 KJB DAGL
PHQ4013

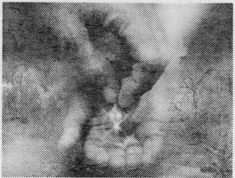